A History *of* the Beanbag

AND OTHER STORIES

About UWA Press New Writing

Since debuting in 2005, the Press's *New Writing* series has attracted the best new fiction authors from Australia and elsewhere. Championed by critics and readers nationwide for their innovative style and challenging subject matter as well as meticulous attention to language and form, the *New Writing* titles are making a sizable contribution to the advancement and enjoyment of quality literature.

Series editor Terri-ann White is actively involved in the literary culture of Australia: as a writer, bookseller, publisher, editor and award judge. Her novel *Finding Theodore and Brina* (2001) is studied in university courses in Spain, the United States and Australia. She published a collection of stories, *Night and Day*, in 1994, has edited anthologies and been published widely. She is currently director of UWA Press and of a cross-disciplinary research centre at The University of Western Australia.

Titles in series

A New Map of the Universe, Annabel Smith
Cusp, Josephine Wilson
The Concerto Inn, Jo Gardiner
The Seamstress, Geraldine Wooller
Paydirt, Kathleen Mary Fallon
The Mystery of the Cleaning Lady, Sue Woolfe
The Last Book You Read, Ewan Morrison
A History of the Beanbag, Susan Midalia

Forthcoming

The Poet Who Forgot, Catherine Cole

A History *of* the Beanbag

AND OTHER STORIES

Susan Midalia

University of Western Australia Press

First published in 2007 by
University of Western Australia Press
Crawley, Western Australia 6009
www.uwapress.uwa.edu.au

We gratefully acknowledge permission to reproduce
extracts from the following:

The Rainbow by D.H. Lawrence, copyright © 1915 by
David Herbert Lawrence, copyright renewed 1943 by
Freida Lawrence. First published by Methuen and Co.,
London. Reproduced with the permission of Pollinger
Limited and the proprietor.

The Life of Art by Helen Garner. Originally appeared in
Postcards From Surfers, copyright © 1985 Helen Garner,
published by Penguin Group Australia Ltd.

While every attempt has been made to obtain permission
to publish all copyright material, if for any reasons a
request has not been received, the copyright holder
should contact the publisher.

National Library of Australia
Cataloguing-in-Publication entry:

Midalia, Susan.
The history of the beanbag: and other stories.
ISBN 978 0 9802965 0 1 (PBK.).
I. Title.
A 823.4

Cover photograph by Joel Maley;
Photograph of the author by Harry Midalia

Edited by Linda Martin
Cover design by Anna Maley-Fadgyas
Series design by Robyn Mundy
Typeset in 10 pt Janson by Lasertype
Printed by McPherson's Printing Group

To Dan, Jack and Harry

Contents

A history of the beanbag

In the history of more recent fads and fashions, the newest, the latest, the hip and the funky, the ephemera of the pop-phenomenal, one could single out any number of ludicrous, shriek-worthy, 'What *were* we thinking?' objects or items of apparel. Women's clothing, for example: hot pants, the poncho, witches britches and platform shoes. For men: body shirts, safari suits, winklepickers, velvet flares. The sartorially improbable and preposterous; so much lust and longing on display. The transience of objects: the lava lamp, with its sleepy gloopy globules; hoola hoops and yoyos; coloured canisters in diminishing sizes, marked F for flour, S for sugar, R for rice, C for coffee; ashtrays shaped like whales, with a hole in the top for the smoke to drift through in grey, lazy swirls.

Let us take one particular item from a random sample of the cool and the kitsch and see where it might lead us. The beanbag, for instance. What histories, both micro- and macrocosmic, might lie within this loose, baggy monster, this faux-bohemian formlessness, in denim, velvet, corduroy or fur? What stories might be summoned, what stories evoked?

Origins

The first beanbag chair was created by the Italian designers Gatti, Paolini and Teodora, whose suavely cosmopolitan names must surely have imparted a glamorous patina to their product. These gentlemen were employed by the Zanotta Company in 1969 when they invented—if that's the right word—the item in question. Think of this: a moment of inspiration (all three at once?) followed by the unstinting application of technological know-how: months of designerly false starts, delays and frustrations, hours and hours of machinists filling, stitching and zipping, factory bosses musing, muttering and scratching their heads, wondering whether this would ever see the light of day. In the end, it was a triumph of ideas, capital and manual labour, working harmoniously together for the benefit of all.

But the origins of the beanbag may have been altogether different. Popular mythology has it that the beanbag came into being as the result of an accident, in which workers in a Styrofoam factory put all the leftover pieces from the production line into a bag and—hey presto—found that they had made a chair which, for the first time, would move with the person sitting in it, would mould itself obligingly to the shifting contours, moods and desires of the human body. This seems a much more appealing version more magically serendipitous, more worthily proletarian. No doubt someone has recorded somewhere a further and detailed history of manufacture, marketing and distribution of the beanbag, but no one seems to know if those putative workers ever profited from their discovery.

Purchase

It is 1974. The place is near a university, more specifically, a share house on a broad, leafy street. Picture a young student named Robyn, about nineteen or twenty. Fairly nondescript in appearance: average height and weight, shoulder-length brown hair, the mandatory T-shirt and jeans. Middle-class, comfortable. She's an earnest young woman aiming to be a social worker, currently studying psychology, maths (for the statistics) and archaeology (for the intellectual pleasure). It doesn't cost much for her to live. The government has just abolished university fees, she rides a bike and her parents help her out from time to time. It's not altogether surprising, then, that on a Wednesday morning at ten o'clock, she wakes up, looks out at the sunny sky and, stretching her arms, says sleepily to herself:

'Today I'm going to buy a beanbag.'

Robyn has never sat in a beanbag and has only seen them through shop windows. Nor does she have a specific need for one. There are seven chairs in her share house, plus one rather ugly but entirely serviceable sofa. But because the day is ahead of her, because her body would like to be enveloped and simply because she can, she decides to buy a beanbag. She has in fact seen two of them, one a purple velvet, the other a coarse cotton weave in pink, spreading nonchalantly on the floor of the local op. shop. Already out of fashion and discarded, but invitingly floppy and flippant. Robyn likes the idea of what she imagines will be something soft and yielding, which will move with her body; something comforting.

She briefly considers asking Kathy to go with her but assumes she's still asleep, and probably not alone. Kathy moved in a month ago, from the country, and is training to be a teacher. She's also gorgeous, with what are coyly and predictably called *bedroom eyes*, although she seems surprisingly unaware of her attractiveness to men. With her flawless complexion and (unfashionable) curves, she's a free advertisement for the benefits of fresh country air and full-cream milk. Glen and Barry certainly noticed the curves when Kathy turned up to answer the ad for a place in the share house. They couldn't take their eyes off her as they fussed about getting her a chair, offering her a coffee. And when she spoke in her shy, quiet voice, they moved in close, not to listen to what she said but to feel the brush of her arm or even the curve of a breast. Robyn was amused by the spectacle of these two confident males, with their private school/born-to-rule swagger, now reduced to puppies, tailwaggingly eager to please. She isn't sure now which one is sleeping with Country Kathy, as she's taken to calling her in her head. She doesn't mean to be unkind, and in fact she quite likes Kathy, who is unassuming and sweet, in a rural kind of way, and who, unlike the boys, does her fair share of work around the house.

Robyn doesn't talk much to her, but she remembers coming home one night to what she thought was an empty house and hearing Kathy singing in her room. To Robyn's untrained ear, this country girl sounded beautiful, indeed exquisite; the notes were low and melancholy, quite unlike the timorous sweetness of her speaking voice. Robyn was surprised at how well she sang, how—haunting, she would have to call it—her tone, and later told her so. Kathy blushed and was tongue-tied, but after some prompting, revealed that she was taking lessons in the blues.

'I know it should probably be country and western,' she smiled self-mockingly, 'but I was really taken with Billie Holiday and Ella Fitzgerald from the time I was a little kid. I'd rather be a blues singer than a teacher any day, but what can you do?' She paused, her bedroom eyes looking suddenly apprehensive. 'Please don't tell anyone, especially Glen. I don't want people thinking I'm big-headed.'

4

After that, Kathy was happy to sing in the house, as long as the boys weren't around.

Robyn is clearly not the romantic heroine of this story. She's aware that men tend not to notice her, and if they do, it's usually merely to confide to her their romantic woes. They can spot her a mile away—smiling openly, a plain, well-meaning fountain of good will, quietly bubbling away in a corner. They assume she likes to go home at the end of a party, sober and alone, feeling good about her role as conciliator or consoler in some affair of the heart. It does, in fact, sometimes please Robyn to know that she's been useful in this way, but she also finds such goodness has its limits. It often makes conversations with men drearily predictable. It confirms to her that she is regarded as a means to an end. So as she walks to the local op. shop, Robyn thinks that buying a beanbag will cheer her up, add some colour to her life. She regards it as a joyfully spontaneous, if rather self-indulgent, act.

In the op. shop, Robyn tries both the purple and the pink. The young guy in the store tells her there's an art to getting into a beanbag and she follows his instructions, first taking it by the top and shaking it round, letting the beans drop more or less evenly to the bottom, then sinking herself in, moving around to adjust. She likes the feeling: it's just as she'd imagined, cosy and enclosing. She decides to buy the purple velvet because it's bigger, big enough for two. For just one moment Robyn wonders whether she should ask the guy to help her take it home, but he doesn't look up from the cash register as she waits for her change. So while it's a bit of a struggle to carry it by herself, it's worth it to see the bemused smiles of her housemates, now showered and dressed, as she stuffs and pushes the unobliging beanbag through the doorway. Glen immediately grabs Kathy by the arm and throws her into it, then jumps on top of her, tickling her furiously all over. It's clear to Robyn that the beanbag is a hit.

Over the next month, Glen is assiduous in his wooing of Kathy. He wants to remove what he calls her 'rough edges' by taking her to nightclubs and bars. 'I'll show you the hotspots,' he grins at her, looking down at his crotch. Kathy misses the look and the joke but nevertheless agrees to be taken in hand. She and Glen spend more and more time out of the house, partying and drinking with his rugby mates. Glen likes the way men look at his girlfriend and the way they call him *a lucky dog*. He's studying commerce and knows enough to know that the more men look at her, the more she's worth. When they stay in for the evening, they often sit together in the beanbag. Once Robyn thinks she sees them having sex in it, but she can't be sure, and in any case, she doesn't want to embarrass them, or herself. And she doesn't want to claim ownership of the beanbag; it's a share house, after all.

Robyn and Kathy hardly meet at all these days. Their paths rarely cross. Barry moves out—Robyn suspects he's tired of watching Glen *slobbering all over Kathy*, as he puts it—and they decide not to advertise for another tenant. Glen says money's not an issue and generously offers to pay the difference in their rent. Most evenings now Robyn is alone and has her beanbag to herself. She's quite content to sit reading, watching TV or listening to the Billie Holiday record she bought Kathy for her birthday.

Clever marketing
It's 1983. The beanbag is making a comeback after several years in decline. Derided for its 1970s hippie associations, it's fast

becoming a serviceable item for more conservative couples. Clever marketing has changed its image from freewheeling free love to something 'indispensable for the kiddies'. Beanbags are comfy for the little ones to sit in while watching TV. They are portable: they can be kept in the rumpus room, away from the good furniture, and stored in a cupboard if required. They're cheap and ultimately disposable. Of course there's the safety issue: the beans can fall out of a bag which hasn't been properly zipped, or older children can find ways to undo the bag when no one is looking. In fact, there's been talk of a fatality: a two-year-old is reported to have choked after ingesting a number of loose beans. While manufacturers and distributors denounce this unverified story, they nevertheless stress the importance of parental vigilance.

Kathy, a much more likely romantic heroine, is in search of her first beanbag, one that's suitable for the child she is carrying. Kathy has been married to Glen for five years. She's never met anyone like him before: such confidence, such self-belief. When she'd lost her virginity to him, it had meant a pledge of some kind. Glen, however, was pleased because he was the first man to have her; he'd *had her cherry*, as he told his mates one night at the pub. Kathy has never taken up teaching, although she did finish her degree. She was married shortly after graduating and Glen had said there was no need for her to work. Besides, they were both keen to start a family. His parents and sister liked her enormously; they thought she was a refreshing change from the rather *rough trade* Glen seemed to have latched onto when he first went to uni. Kathy was shy, of course, and a little overwhelmed by their house: she'd never been inside a place with a games room and three bathrooms, each one blinding white, and a separate dining room with upholstered jarrah chairs. There wasn't a beanbag in sight. But the family made her feel at home and she learnt not to feel too silly when she wrapped herself up in one of their jumbo-sized towels or sat on the Chesterfield settee, carefully balancing a cup of tea on her lap.

So it's with a light heart that Kathy walks, or rather sways, to the furniture store to buy a beanbag. She and Glen already have a house full of tapestried chairs, leather settees and embroidered *chaises-longues* (she'd never heard this word before until her mother-in-law took her shopping), but she likes the idea of something a little more informal, something for a child, even a little childish. Of course Glen is only too happy to indulge her whim. Kathy has seen beanbags in the windows of children's stores and has fallen in love with their sheer tinyness, their endearing pear-shape, their colourful patterns. This purchase, she knows, is an act of faith in the future, in the arrival of the healthy baby she and Glen have longed for so much. She has had two miscarriages, distressing and difficult to forget, both at three months; but now she is nearly to term, and this baby is kicking, turning somersaults, full of life. Kathy wants her beanbag to be the most vibrant one in the store. She's happily talked into a rather expensive one, purple velvet with the faces of Bert and Ernie on it, and it's only later she recalls that it's exactly the same deep purple of the beanbag from her student days. She remembers that it belonged to one of the housemates and how they'd all laughed when she'd struggled with it through the door. She hasn't seen Robyn—that was her name—for many years now, not since her wedding, and has no idea what's become of her. Kathy recalls that the girl was kind to her when she moved into the share house; she showed her round the campus and sometimes talked with her. She remembers that Robyn liked her singing, but that was a long time ago.

A decline in standards

Three years have passed; it's 1986. Kathy and Glen's daughter is also called Kathy, at her father's insistence. He sees this as a testament to his beautiful wife, with whom he is still very much in love (his mates sometimes remind him of what a *lucky dog* he is). Despite her protestations, he has his way about the name. Glen dotes on his daughter and likes to watch her belly flop into her purple beanbag. He laughs, but he's also careful, aware of the perilous pleasures this item affords. Kathy junior is all the more precious because she was a long time in the making. She was no accident.

It worries Glen that lately his wife seems to be taking less interest in their daughter than she should. It was fine when Kathy junior was a baby; her mother adored her, and would spend hours singing to her, songs like 'Incy Wincy Spider' and some odd, sad numbers that he didn't know. But now, he notices, Kathy is spending more on babysitters and going out more than she used to. She tells him she's meeting friends for lunch and that Kathy junior is too young to take to the expensive restaurants the girls seem to like. Glen isn't entirely convinced. His wife's still a very good-looking woman; he sees the way men look at her, ogling her really, and now that she's a mother, he feels it isn't right. Nevertheless he gives her the benefit of the doubt. He thinks that his wife doesn't smell like a woman who's having sex with another man. He reminds her that she's always promised they'd try for another baby. He's very keen to have a second, preferably a son.

Things worsen during the year. Glen sees that his wife is drinking more than her share of wine in the evenings and he even suspects her of drinking during the day. Once or twice he smells alcohol on her breath, when he knows she hadn't planned to go out. She seems absent-minded, sort of dreamy. She's put on some weight, but he finds the extra curves sexy and is surprised at her blank face when he tells her so. One day he comes home from work to find her singing in the shower, while their child is alone in the rumpus room, diving into the beanbag, her face smothered with laughter. Next he discovers a pile of unpaid bills for—of all things—weekly singing lessons. Glen is perturbed and puts a stop to it. It's not that he minds the money, not at all; it's the neglect of his child, the secrecy and the sheer pointlessness of it all. He tells his wife that another baby will fix whatever's wrong with her.

What finally outrages him—it's the turning point in this story—is the day he comes home to find Kathy asleep, dead drunk, on their bed, while his daughter sits in another room in the beanbag, crying, with her lap full of a plate of baked beans. She tells him between sobs that she's been stuck in the beanbag *for a long time, Daddy*. Glen rouses his wife and raises his voice, drowning out her slurred and cowed defence. Released by her father from the beanbag and now safely asleep in her bed, Kathy junior doesn't hear her father's words echoing, booming, in the master bedroom.

Narrative destinations

Fast forward some years. It's 1994 and we're back at the same broad, leafy street where Robyn brought home the purple beanbag all those years ago. The share house has been demolished and replaced by a row of four neat, tree-shaded apartments. One of them belongs to Robyn, now a social worker. Like the other dwellings, hers has polished floorboards, high ceilings and built-in bookshelves, in which there is no longer any room for the many books she has accumulated, and read, over the years. Her furniture is modest, eclectic: wicker and cane chairs, an old jarrah dining table with a hand-embroidered tablecloth from Brazil, where she worked for three years; a purple cotton weave sofa with scatter cushions in various shades of blue. There is also a beanbag, the latest in a succession of them. Robyn has retained an affection for these Saccos, as they were originally called, beyond the vagaries of fads and fashions. They remind her of her relatively carefree uni days, with their attendant privileges and pleasures. She enjoys their accommodating hollows, the comfort of a place in which to sink down, with a book, immersed in silence and solitude.

Not that Robyn is lonely. While she's lived alone for many years and has never married, she has several cherished nephews and nieces and a number of precious friends, as well as a lover of some ten years whom she meets often for outings to concerts and films, for dinner and conversation. He's a Professor of archaeology who lives a few streets away. When he visits Robyn in her apartment, or stays overnight, he knows her well enough to know that he mustn't sit in her beanbag, which is only big enough for one. This is the one object to which she lays claim, which she wants entirely to herself.

This afternoon Robyn is sitting in her newest beanbag—it's a couple of years old, corduroyed, already wearing a little thin. She chose it for the nostalgia of psychedelic pink and because it clashes with the other colours in her living room. She's taken the day off work—a rare occurrence—because she's in need of a break. She's close to sleep, feeling drowsy after hours of slopping around in her dressing-gown, eating when the mood takes her and reading trashy magazines. Not that she's a complainer or malingerer. Indeed, she remains buoyantly optimistic about people, despite years of contact with what her concerned mother, at the beginning of her daughter's career, called *the seedy side of life* and *the dregs of humanity*. Certainly, Robyn has seen much to give her cause for cynicism or despair. She once sang satirically to a friend, imitating Barbra Streisand in full voice, 'People who need social workers are the unluckiest people in the world.' The poor, the embittered, the battered, the homeless, the sick, the deranged. But she also believes, from first-hand observation, from listening, that most suffering is the product of ignorance or thoughtlessness rather than deliberate cruelty. This belief is what's kept her going.

As she drifts off into an indulgent sleep, she hears singing from the apartment next door. This isn't unusual: Jodie is a music teacher who gives private lessons, mainly to high-school students. Most afternoons between three and six, Robyn can hear wafting through her walls various scales, tunes, songs from young hopefuls or those coerced by ambitious parents. She's seen one or two of the students leaving, carrying heavy schoolbags, young kids in uniform on their way home, no doubt, to more lessons, perhaps to more coercion. But this afternoon is different. The voice Robyn hears is adult, and arresting. She can't make out the lyrics but the melody is sweetly melancholy, rather haunting. She finds herself fully awake, attentive, wanting to hear more.

The singing lasts for the prescribed half an hour and when it's over, Robyn finds her curiosity piqued. She struggles out of her beanbag and moves to the window, parting the curtains, feeling like one of those gossiping biddies she sometimes encounters in her work and whom she secretly loathes. She sees a woman coming out of Jodie's door—a blonde, about forty years old; attractive, quite stunning in fact. And then Robyn recognises her. Kathy, Country Kathy, who married that rugby player and who was such a happy young woman, a girl really, way back when. She hasn't seen her since her wedding—how many years ago?—but this is unmistakably Kathy. Her face, that most individualising of features, is the same: a peaches-and-cream complexion, those *bedroom eyes*, that air of rural innocence. She remembers, too, Kathy's voice, and how she would only ever sing when the boys weren't home; and before she can stop herself, she goes outside and offers a greeting:

'Kathy? Remember me? Robyn—Robyn from the share house in Forrestdale, back in the seventies. You used to sing the blues; and you married Glen. How are you?'

Kathy looks up, startled, and Robyn can feel herself being sized up, as if the woman is unsure of her, suspicious. She's seen this look many times before—from the wary, the damaged, the vengeful, who think the social worker is just another person who will do them over, do them in. But then Kathy smiles shyly, with recognition.

'Robyn. Why, of course—my goodness, that *was* a long time ago. When did we last meet? My wedding, I think it was.'

There is the predictable awkward silence, in which smiles are momentarily forced, as both women inwardly register the gap of twenty years. They know there could be so much to say, or nothing at all. Surprisingly, it's Kathy who speaks first:

'Ah yes, my wedding. Glen and I divorced a while back— seven years ago. We have a daughter, Kathy, she's eleven.' She pauses, her face clouded. 'I wish she had her own name, but what can you do? She lives with her father, but I see her on weekends and we get on—well, really fine.'

Kathy looks at Robyn's face and sees in it an invitation to disclosure. She sees, not the practised expression of the experienced social worker, disinterested and calmly professional, but the eyes of someone who seems, genuinely, to want to know.

'It's hard, of course, but it was the right thing to do. I wasn't the best of mothers, you know. I wanted to be, I love my daughter, but somehow I became unhappy and I started drinking and not looking after her properly.' She wonders how she might tell her story. 'But things are better now. And Glen's a good dad, he really is, but he's still—well, angry, about many things. It's hard, for some people, to forgive.'

Her words seem suddenly weighted, but then her voice, her rather thin, unmelodious speaking voice, resumes. 'I don't drink anymore and—well, I guess you heard me—I've started taking singing lessons again.'

'I remember.' Robyn smiles brightly with reminiscence. 'You always liked to sing the blues—when we were alone in the house. Do you have any plans—a career in mind?'

Kathy screws up her face and then laughs.

'A career? Oh no, no, nothing like that. I just love the music, I suppose. And because—well, I just want to get better, to be the best I can.'

Robyn remembers why, so long ago, she'd liked Kathy: because she was unassuming and sincere. And then, because it seems entirely right, this looping back to a new beginning, she invites her in for a coffee, ushers her through the doorway and gestures around the room.

'Please, have a seat, Kathy,' she says. 'Sit anywhere you like.'

Freeze frame

People all over the world have their favourite Hollywood moment: an image of desire perhaps, or anguish, desperation or terror. For female fans of *Gone with the Wind*, swooning under the weight of all that satin, there's the first view of the roguish Rhett Butler, smiling at the foot of the stairs. The tenderhearted remember the theatrical gestures of the ravaged Blanche DuBois, piteously self-deluding, shielding her aging face from the naked light. For the ghoulish, there's the unforgettable *Psycho*, still frightening after all these years: Norman Bates's eye in the keyhole, the shadow behind the shower curtain, the bloodied water spiralling down the drain, dissolving into a close-up of the dead woman's open eye.

One of the most popular moments occurs in that most popular of films, *The Wizard of Oz*. That startling instant when the movie changes from black and white to colour, or, more precisely, from the monochromatic drabness of sepia, browns and greys into a blaze of brilliant blues, reds, oranges and yellows. So often cited, analysed, celebrated, by experts and nostalgic amateurs alike, that technicolour transformation is now a movie cliché, so easy to dismiss. But of course, it isn't a cliché when you see it for the very first time, as Annie found when, as a six-year-old, she was taken by her parents to the cinema. She was literally jolted out of her seat by that bedazzling, electrifying movement into colour. She watched, goggle-eyed and gobsmacked, as Dorothy was whirled from the real to the fantastical, from her slow-moving, humdrum home in Kansas to a land of limitless possibilities. Annie's parents, wisely, hadn't told her this would happen, so that she too could be Dorothy, magically transported from her familiar world to a realm of vivid, undreamed-of wonderment, both beautiful and bizarre. For *some* of what happened in the kingdom of Oz was indeed alarming. Bad-tempered trees sprang into life, pelting Dorothy and her hapless friends with apples. More terrifying were the menacing troops of monkeys, with hideously distorted faces, filling up the sky. Worst of all was the Wicked Witch of the East who dissolved into a puddle, shrivelled away, her solid flesh-and-bloodness disappearing before Annie's very eyes. How could this happen, she wondered, aghast, childishly spooked by this macabre disintegration, this bodily melting away.

But with her parents sitting next to her, one on either side, Annie's fears were allayed. She peeped up at her mother or father from time to time to see their reassuring smiles; she leaned over to have her hand held, squeezed gently, in some of the scarier parts. There was also the rallying presence in the cinema of dozens of other excited children, whose communal cheers, boos, gasps and laughter helped to loosen the knots of apprehension in Annie's stomach. And of course in the end, after all the suspense, trepidation and shock, Dorothy found herself back in the warmth of her family, returned to the comfort of the known. So in this snug cinematic cocoon, Annie had the luxury of letting herself go; she was caught up in a dream, bound by a spell. She thought that *movies* was just the right word for *The Wizard of Oz*, which was speedy, dizzy, exhilarating. This was how she experienced it at the time, that sense of whirling movement, and how she remembered it throughout her adult life.

But Annie also had another, altogether different, movie memory from her childhood; one which was repulsive and fearful, one which haunted her for years. If she were asked to recall this other movie, words like *grotesque*, *contaminating*, *dreadful*, would come to mind. She might also say it was like a series of images—of faces, hands, bodies—forever frozen in some ghastly allegorical past. She would say that she was left with pictures in her head which she wished weren't there, and which no amount of adult reasoning or reassurance, no retrospective wisdom, could ever properly dispel.

Annie is eight years old when she's taken by her sister to see a movie—a comedy, she's told, some light entertainment. She's thrilled by the prospect of this rare outing, an afternoon spent with her adored Sophia, who is so much older and so enchanting, with her long golden hair and smooth white skin. Annie hopes that Sophia will help her choose a dress to wear—will it be her best pink one, with the Princess sleeves?—or buy her an ice cream, and bestow on her a regal smile. For above all Annie wants to be noticed by Sophia, to have conferred from on high the gaze of this heavenly sister, who, from a very early age, has appeared to her like the moon, silver-gold and remotely beautiful, way up in the dark night sky.

But as the two of them set out for the cinema, waved off by distant parental injunctions, Annie can see that Sophia looks different, that some mysterious transformation has taken place that day. Her sister is wearing shiny black stockings and high-heeled shoes, slim and sleek, pointed at the toes; her green dress is pulled in tightly at the waist with a black patent-leather belt. And her face is different too. Annie sees it from below, a glowing face: pink cheeks, silver-sparkly eyelids and the brightest of red lips. Sophia appears to her newly wrapped and newly coloured; she is like a film star, all glamorous and glossy, like the posters Annie has seen on her sister's bedroom wall.

Annie remembers arriving at the cinema and descending a steep flight of stairs, leaving the sunlight of the daytime world. She can remember that heady sensation of walking, almost float-ing down, with the illuminated Sophia at her side. There's some chatter in the foyer below, people milling about, sharp bursts of laughter. Children are eating popcorn, throwing pieces up in the air, catching them in wide-open mouths. Annie can see people looking up at them as she and Sophia descend the stairs, and she feels important, so grand, so grateful to her sister for making this happen, for making this entrance together. She almost expects to hear a fanfare, or see cameras flashing their bulbs, hear a voice saying, *Look this way, ladies, just one more picture, please.*

It's then that Annie sees the next face, a man's face, below her in the middle-distance. She remembers it as dark and thin, with shadows under the eyes, and she doesn't know whether it is handsome or ugly. She catches the smile the man gives to Sophia as he stands waiting at the foot of the stairs. Her sister with the bright red lips stops, her hands on her hips, and then moves close to the dark man, who could be handsome or ugly, and who looks older, much older even than Sophia, because of the way he smiles. Annie watches the two of them laughing together, and more and more she begins to feel like she is not really there. Sophia says something to her and the man buys her an ice cream, but she knows instinctively that she is being moved to one side. In the brightly lit foyer, where everything seems both sharply outlined and oddly unreal, it's as if she has become a pair of watching eyes. Annie sees certain things in close-up: the man's mouth, which is shiny with moisture, and which brushes the back of Sophia's neck. Her sister's pale white flesh, glistening in the place where the man's mouth has been. A green dress, which has become so bright that Annie has to look away.

Now they are in a dark room, where Annie can dimly make out rows and rows of seats with little glowing dots at the ends to help them find their way. She remembers Sophia laughing, even though the film hasn't started, and she is aware of something moving next to her. She sees it is the man's hand, thick and dark, on her sister's thigh. He is sliding it up and down Sophia's shiny stockings, and Annie feels suddenly afraid; for herself or her sister, she cannot tell. Pictures appear on the screen but she is only half-watching, because she can see out of the corner of her eye that Sophia and the man have their faces close together, and that his hand is still moving, slowly, up and down. Annie feels a tightness in her chest.

It is then, at that precise moment, that she turns her gaze from the moving hand to the screen in front of her. She closes her eyes quickly but it's too late. No one told her not to look. An image swims up to her, a slow dissolve in reverse, a picture which makes Annie feel that her entire body is full of some foul liquid. It is an image, in grainy black and white, of a dead woman lying face-up in the mud. To Annie she looks like an alien creature: her naked body is bloated, her face is at an angle and hideously distorted, and she is staring, staring out at no one, her eyes puffed out like mad and monstrous balloons. Annie feels as if the awful stuff inside her will pour out from her mouth, all over the floor, her lacy pink dress. She has to fight back a lurching sensation, clutching on to the sides of her chair, trying to keep everything inside.

For some time after—she has no idea how long—Annie knows that things are going on around her, happening without her. She senses the presence of other people, hears occasional bursts of laughter, sees the flickering of a movie on a screen. But for the rest of that afternoon she feels as though time has stopped, the world has stopped, at that particular moment, when a woman's body rose up from the mud, dreadfully, grotesquely, unalive. Annie remembers re-emerging into the cruel light of the foyer: it is a painful light, making her eyes smart with tears. She sees the man's arm around Sophia's waist. She sees her sister's face, shiny and magnified, more flushed and glowing than before. Her hair is messy, falling in wild swirls, and her bright red lips are smudged into a gash. She appears to Annie like a doll, a silly, painted, crumpled doll, who hardly looks like Sophia at all.

For several years, Annie's parents tried to laugh away this incident, this moment in her childhood when they were not there, when so much was disturbing and inexplicably wrong. They would remind her, a little teasingly, of that afternoon when she came home in a silent sulk and wouldn't talk to her sister for weeks. It was some time before Annie could speak about the picture of the woman, the dead woman in the mud. Her parents tried to put her mind at rest, describing what she'd seen as a newsreel, a story about a notorious crime. It was only recently, they told her, that the corpse had been identified and that, thankfully, the police had caught the man who'd hurt the woman and left her for dead. Her parents claimed this as a victory for forensic science, determination and justice, but Annie found their explanation brutally unconsoling. She never did tell them about the unknown man who seemed to have disappeared, as if by magic, without a trace, from her sister's life. All that Annie was left with, what would never go away, were those pictures: a man waiting at the foot of the stairs; a thick hand on a stockinged thigh; a bloated corpse staring out from the mud; and Sophia's slashed red mouth, as she returned her sister, bereft and betrayed, into the daylight world.

Legless

Those boys had come round to see his brother again. Marty didn't like them much, he hated them actually, because they shouted and screamed and made a noise like donkeys when they watched TV. And because they said dirty words and drank beer, without ever stopping. He didn't know who they were, just that they showed up a lot, hanging round on Saturdays, sometimes Sundays too. To Marty, these boys had a strange kind of darkness. Although they were all light-coloured, with yellow hair streaked by the sun, pale faces and flat blue eyes, there was something about the way they laughed which Marty knew was dark. They thought he didn't know things, but he could hear a rumbling noise, low and secret, underneath their laughing, like they were waiting for something to happen. Their darkness was different from the one in his bedroom, which was cool and comforting, and where he didn't do much except lie on his bed and think about things he liked and didn't like.

He liked the garden his mum had built out the front, with lots of leaves and sort of bellflowers twirling over the fence, and in the ground she'd put things that looped around or bunched up together or stretched up to the sky, in pale pinks and blues and real bright oranges. Marty liked them all, every one of them. Nothing screamed at him here. His mum had taken a long time to make their garden because she could only buy one thing a week. A few times Marty had pinched cuttings from the neighbours' front yard, even though his mum had told him not to. He thought they'd never know, and anyway he didn't like them because of how they looked at his mum, or just looked away. There used to be trees in the back garden but now there was only a big log left over from when they were chopped down. The man behind the fence made his mum do it because he said the trees messed up his pool. His mum didn't want to but he'd heard the man tell her, in a dark voice, that he'd *call the council* and he had *a son who would come round and talk to her.*

Now that their trees were gone, Marty looked at the ones across the street. In the daytime these trees had long white trunks with blotches of brown on them like someone had painted them, and branches bursting with leaves. At night in his cool dark room, when it was that still you could hear yourself breathing, Marty stared at the trees 'til he could hear the branches singing. And he could *see* the singing too, it was like the glass blown by that man in the mall, the man Marty liked to stand and watch for a long time, who spun out the glass 'til it looked like silver fairy floss and then he turned it into sailing ships and swans. And in the garden Marty liked to watch things move—the beetles, the spiders and the snails, with their different ways of getting from one place to another or just hanging around, turning in circles or nibbling at leaves. The ants were his favourite because they ran around like crazy and because they were really strong, carrying bits of food like they'd just unloaded them from a ship, like his dad used to do. The ants carried little parcels of bread and meat and sometimes Marty fed them cake crumbs as a treat. And most of all he liked his mum, for so many things that he couldn't remember them all, so many that he couldn't hold them in his head. Her soft hands on his face and how she held him to her chest when he was afraid, and how she sat with him on the log and watched the ants. How she held his hand when she walked him to school and when she walked him home again. And all the stories she told him, that she just made up in her own head. These were just some of the things. And he liked her even more now that his dad was gone, because there was more of her when she stood up straight and when she laughed.

Then there were the things he didn't like, which made him all hot inside and made him hit things, hit himself, or just cry. He didn't like the TV because it screamed at him and no one was allowed to turn it off, ever. Trev got mad if he or his mum tried to turn it off, even if no one was watching. Often when Marty got up at night, when he was the only one awake, there were lights from the screen flickering everywhere and when he stopped in the middle of the room and looked around it felt like being in another place, in outer space, where it was silent except for a dark hum and where it felt like he was the only thing alive. It felt like there was nothing there at all. When he stood there, in outer space, he felt afraid first, and then the sad feeling came and the tears would run down his face. Marty didn't like playing sport either because his arms got in the way. He could never catch the balls and then kids shouted at him and when he ran he fell over and hurt himself so he wouldn't have to play anymore. He didn't like school either, because of everything.

Most of all he hated these boys for coming into their lives, his and his mum's, for just being there. Last week two of them had sicked up on the carpet in the lounge room. Marty and his mum had tried to get the smell out with a sponge cloth and his mum had even brought home a carpet machine from the shops, but the stink was still there, except now the sick was mixed up with the shampoo. It was a kind of sad smell, Marty thought. It made his mum sad, even though she tried not to show it because she didn't want to make Trev mad. Marty knew it probably wasn't a nice thing to say, or even think, but he didn't like his brother. He didn't like the way he shouted at their mum and the way he watched TV all the time and he didn't like the dirty white foam on his mouth when he drank beer and the stubbly bits of hair on his chin, which Trev would scratch and scratch, real slow, when he looked at you. Sometimes he'd laugh at Marty and call him a girl. *Bloody girl. Bloody poofter.* Or *Retard.* And most of all he hated those boys. He hated the way they would push him a bit when they walked past him. He hated their big bellies and the way they talked, all loud and slurry, and he hated the way they pulled the ring on their beer cans and tilted their heads back and said *Jeeze, that's good,* and then belched and laughed.

This Saturday, when the boys came round, there was the new one again, the one who'd been round the week before. He was called Wil and he had big black marks all over his arms and shoulders. Marty knew these marks were called tattoos because his dad had one, only his was small, it was a heart with an arrow through it. Wil's tattoos were so big you couldn't see his real skin, just lots of black dragons and animals Marty had never seen before, animals with horns and fangs, so it looked like Wil's arms and shoulders were full of crawling things, things that twisted round and round and ate each other up. It didn't matter where you were standing in the lounge room, you could see the animals crawling up and down his arms. Marty could see his mum's face when Wil walked through the door, her face sort of dropped. She said she'd make some lunch like she was trying to be nice to them but Marty knew she wanted to get away from the tattoos and because he'd seen how last time Wil had grabbed her, when Marty had heard him say *Great tits, Val*, and laugh in a low voice, and then laugh again when his mum pushed him off. Tits was a dirty word, ugly, like Wil. It made Marty think of pus. So he didn't go into his room like he usually did. Instead he followed his mum into the kitchen and stood there watching her get out the bread from the plastic bag and cutting it into thick slices and spreading the margarine with her hands working fast, like she was in a hurry to go somewhere.

From the kitchen Marty could see the boys lying all over the couch and he could hear them making a lot of noise in front of the TV and singing like they were supposed to be happy. Marty knew it was the cricket because they were calling out *Pommies are wankers*, in these singing kinds of voices. *POM-ies are WANK-ers*, with some parts louder than others. Marty knew that Pommies meant their dad as well as the cricket because Trev used to shout out the words even louder than normal when he and their dad watched TV, just to make their dad mad. One of the boys, the one called Les, had his beer can stuck to his mouth and he was leaning back his head so much you thought it would break off. Another one, whose name Marty didn't know, the one who was always scratching himself, looked real hard down the hole in the top of his can, like he was trying to find something. Then Trev shouted out to Marty in the kitchen, 'Hey kid, bring us some more beer, will ya?'

Marty saw his mum keep on cutting the bread and her hands were getting faster and she was digging the knife harder. She didn't look up, she just kept looking at the bread and she said to Trev:

'Why don't you get up and get it yourself? Marty's not your slave.'

Trev's voice was like next door's dog yapping and snapping. 'The dumbarse isn't doin' nothin', he can make 'imself useful.'

Then Wil jumped up from the couch like he'd just woken up and said, all cheerful, 'Don't worry, mate, I'll get it', and he walked over to the kitchen, with his big belly spilling over the belt in his trousers. His belly was all sloppy and spongy, like you could poke things into it and they'd sink right in and never come back. Marty saw Wil bend down and open the fridge door and then he was standing right next to his mum, right close to her. He saw all the animals on Wil's arms curling and swirling round his mum's stomach, squeezing her a bit hard, and then Wil put his head on her neck. Marty saw his mum whirl round real fast and point her knife in Wil's stomach. She just kept it pressed there and said, 'If you touch me again, you'll be real sorry.' His mum's voice was low, but not dark, it was straight and strong like the trees across the street. Wil looked a bit funny, kind of surprised, and then he walked out of the kitchen, his feet heavy, like he was marching somewhere.

'Let's sit in the garden, baby,' Marty heard his mum saying. She plonked the cut-up bread and the knife down hard and took Marty's hand. When they were outside Marty could hear her taking big breaths, see her chest move up and down. She led him over to the log and sat down, patting a space beside her. He always liked it when his mum did this, making this space for him, and then leaning against him, tilting her head and pointing to things in the garden. He could hear her voice saying the names of flowers. They were all names he liked, that he could almost say with her because he'd heard them so many times. *Marigolds.*

Geraniums. Petunias. Columbines. Then they watched the ants together and his mum told him stories about what they were doing. *This one's packed to go on a holiday to Mexico,* she said. And then she told him about Mexico and how empty it was and how red, red all over. *And this one's going to see the King of France. See how big and important he looks.*

And then Marty spotted something moving in the grass, the long grass by the fence. He could see something sort of silvery grey, like the colour of his dad's old car, all shiny, catching the sun. He pointed to it and he and his mum got off the log and she made him wait behind her while she walked real slow, on her tiptoes, nearer to the fence. She looked down at the silvery patch and then she waved to Marty to come over, saying, *Sh, sh, sh,* putting her finger on her mouth. She looked real excited, her face all opened up. 'Look, baby, it's a legless lizard', she said, keeping him back from this strange long thin thing he'd never seen before. 'It's OK, it won't hurt you', she said, looking at his face. 'It's not gunna bite. Let's just look at it.' So they did, just stood there, looking at how smooth and slippery and shiny it was, all long and slithery like a snake, *but they don't bite,* his mum said. The lizard was so quiet, just lying there, so peaceful in the sun. It had a real tiny head and the rest of it was a long ribbon with the light bouncing off it. He wanted his mum to tell him a story about it.

Then there was a noise behind them. It was Wil, but Marty and his mum hadn't seen him coming, or heard him coming, and now he was here. 'What ya lookin' at?' he said, all sloppy in his voice. Marty's mum turned round and took a breath and moved away a bit from Wil.

'It's a legless lizard,' she told him, just like she'd told Marty, only now she sounded sad.

'A bloody legless lizard!' Wil looked at Marty's mum like the teacher sometimes did, kind of friendly but not friendly. Marty could see the tattoos on Wil's arms and smell the beer, it was all over him, like the black animals all over his skin.

'Well fuck me dead! What's it bloody doin' round 'ere?' Marty's mum just turned her back on him and kept looking at the lizard. Then Wil started shouting, like out of nowhere, throwing his arms in the air, making black swirls in Marty's face. 'What the fuck's it doin' here, just crawlin round on its belly, doesn't belong here, stupid fuckin' bloody legless lizard!' And then he laughed real loud, holding on to his stomach. 'Bloody legless, that's a good one!' Marty's mum turned round and gave Wil a bit of a shove and looked at him real close up and said, 'It's got just as much right to be here as you do, more bloody right in fact. Just piss off, will ya, and leave us alone.'

Then Wil did the dark thing. He grabbed the shovel that was leaning on the fence and swung it over his head and kept swinging it and swinging it like he could hardly hold on and then he smashed it down onto the lizard, he just kept smashing it and breaking it up into lots of little pieces, there were silver bits flying everywhere. Marty could hear his mum sort of moaning and then she started pushing Wil hard, pushing against him, only he didn't move, and then Wil dropped the shovel and grabbed her and started running his hands all over her, real hard and fast all over and Marty could see him breathing real fast and he was saying, 'Come on, Val, ya know you want it, you know ya want it.' And Marty could see his mum's face all red and crying and her hands banging against Wil's stomach and then he saw Wil fall down into the grass, his legs just crumpled from under him and he was lying there all slumped over. So Marty picked up the shovel at Wil's feet and started banging

Wil's legs with the shiny edge, the edge that was all sharp and silver and beautiful because it was catching the light of the sun. Wil couldn't move or stand up, he was just lying there, so Marty kept chopping and chopping and looking at the blood he'd made, dark and deep, red and beautiful, all over Wil's legs. He could hear some whooping sounds coming from the house and then he saw all the other boys running towards them, Trev in front, screaming. Marty knew his mum was still crying and he could see the lizard lying in little silver pieces all over the grass, and there were lots of drops of red on the ground, bright red and real tiny, like the bits of confetti his mum had found in their garden a long time ago. She'd told him once, a long time ago, that confetti meant people being happy.

It's only words

Ever since I can remember, I've been in the business of language. Not, it must be understood, in the sense or spirit of commerce. Nothing as crassly literal as dollars per word or page, nothing as vulgar as awards, competitions or grants, advances, promotions or prizes. Rather, I love the *busy-ness* of language. I feel myself to be, always and everywhere, immersed in, enamoured of, embraced by, words, words, words. I'm an inveterate reader of novels (both canonical and contemporary), of poetry, stories, essays, biographies, autobiographies, historical treatises, philosophical tomes. In short, I'm proudly, and generically, promiscuous. I adore, too, the physicality of language, its saturation of the everyday. Wherever I look or listen—on the radio and in shopping malls, on television and in newspapers, on billboards, placards, postcards, magazines, in airports, hotels and waiting rooms—my eyes and ears are open to the wondrousness of words. Hectoring or hieratic, insouciant or ensorcelling, baroque or unadorned; wily, whining, ad-man slick, resonant, redolent, exuberant, turbulent and gorgeous; language, I know, is always, and never simply, *there*.

Sometimes it's the sound of a word that beguiles me. Words which yearn, like *mesmeric* and *mirage*; mellifluous, euphonious. Or consider the jarring, jolting words—those that wound, like *ingratitude*. I've succumbed to the bend of *submission* and been lured by the cool of *hauteur*. *Curmudgeonly*—now, there's a word—niggardly, churlish, miserly—awaiting the curve of *kindness* and *compassion*. Or take my own particular word—*Silvia*. My name, derived from sylvan, of the woods. A Latin word, a silver word, immortalised (such a clichéd word) by Shakespeare (who, it has been calculated, had a vocabulary of some forty thousand words and who is credited with the invention of the word *bubble*).

At other times it is simply the placement of words.

No no no no no.

Sometimes it's the very look of words that, as it were, tickles my fancy. When my friend Helen and I were younger, much younger, we'd meet at the local shopping mall to inspect the verbal bloopers dotted around the stores. We'd laugh explosively at a sighting, feeling childishly superior to the clichés, malapropisms and mixed metaphors on signs and billboards. We particularly enjoyed the greengrocer's blackboard, with its ever-changing, idiosyncratic and ludicrous itemisation of produce. Once Helen shrieked at the sight of *Collieflowers*:

'Look, Sil,' she pointed in delight, 'a vegetable that's gone to the dogs! And *blewberries*—an orgasmic delight.'

Amid the flourish of mad mis-spellings, I spotted the single and singular use of quotation marks to distinguish one particular fruit:

'Bananas'

'Would you look at that!' I expostulated, mock-indignantly. 'Is this, I wonder, a knowingly vulgar Freudian reference to man's crooked tumescence? "Bananas": could this be a sexual wink-and-nudge from Con the Greengrocer—a promise of off-the-premises bliss?'

'You misrepresent the man,' Helen protested. 'This device of punctuation is a sign of something altogether more subtle and sophisticated. He is elevating the fruit into a state of ontological uncertainty. These are not, it would seem, "real" bananas, but tantalisingly textualised, socially constructed, the products of a mediating consciousness, namely, that of Mr Con Albinoni, the philosophical provender.'

We'd always enjoyed this kind of linguistic nonsense, this larking about with words. It was in fact through words and reading that we first met, as students of Eng. Lit., and recognised in each other a giddy infatuation with language. Helen was sprung by the rhythms of Gerard Manley Hopkins and I swooned (albeit in translation) over the assonance in Proust. I was ambushed by the later Joyce's verbal prankstering, while Helen remained unashamedly reverential in the presence of Austen's tripartite sentence structure (modelled, of course, on Dr Johnson's classical prose). There was also the obligatory, posturing self-pity in the wake of reading Eliot, (T.S.). Helen and I would stroll languidly through the lush university gardens, affecting *ennui* (so much more glamorous, more meaningful, than *boredom*), intoning our favourite lines—cultivating the weariness, the entombing dreariness, of growing old, growing old. It was only much later, more or less done with childrearing and certainly done with marriage, that we recognised the absurd inappropriateness, the comic-pathetic undergraduateness, of such words, such gestures. But bookish and snobbish and seventeen, enervated by Antipodean parochialism, we were drawn to the desultory cadences of J. Alfred Prufrock, measuring out his monotonous life of stifled desperation. Quoting Eliot, putting on his mask, made us feel part of a grand literary tradition. It made our misery more rarified and vaguely canonical.

In our second year at university we discovered D.H. Lawrence, the works of. (He was considered *a bit too much* for freshers). Years later we would laugh at our obsession with his descriptions of sex, and confess to being embarrassed by our youthfully feminine blindness to his misogyny, not to mention the turgidness of some of his prose. But we also realised, after having children of our own, how well he wrote about the emotional intensities of parenthood. I remember a phone conversation with Helen after her late-night re-reading of *The Rainbow*. It was that time in her life when her only child had started to grow away from her, when she was pained by her adolescent son's absolute rejection of physical contact. Michael had been one of those joyously demonstrative children, roly-poly and curly haired, forever on the move, who loved being hurled in the air and exuberantly embraced. Even when at a standstill, he wanted to touch. He especially liked his mother's butterfly kisses, when her eyelashes fluttered against his cheeks in a delicate tickling motion. He would giggle and squirm with pleasure and say, *Again*.

'And now,' Helen told me—I could hear the sadness in her voice—'he's transmogrified into this—this, unrecognisable being, this fourteen-year-old stranger, so awkward in his body, unable or unwilling to touch, or be touched, by the mother whose body once enclosed him, who's given him hugs of celebration and consolation and who now feels completely rejected, damn it, so alone and out in the cold.' She paused, reflectively.

'Forgive the self-pity, Sil,' she said. 'It's just that when I re-read Lawrence, it made my sense of loss even more unbearable. Remember the description of little Ursula running to meet her father? Here, I have the book open in front of me…Remember how the child would start to run as soon as she saw him, *would*

34

come running in tiny, wild, windmill fashion, lifting her arms up and down to him, down the steep hill... And here's the really piercing part, when I began to sob... *Once she fell as she came flying to him, he saw her pitch forward suddenly as she was running with her hands lifted to him; and when he picked her up, her mouth was bleeding. He could never bear to think of it, he always wanted to cry, even when he was an old man and she had become a stranger to him.'*

I found myself suddenly thinking of my husband, wondering whether he too would be saddened by such a moment, when he was an old man. I had, after all, taken our children, abandoned him in ways I didn't want to talk about, even think about, just then. Besides, it was Helen who'd called to say she was unhappy. I knew that my words would keep for another time.

And of course, in a friendship of such enduring literariness, there was the question of our names, both of which, we knew, placed us firmly in the tradition of High Culture.

'My parents were not, and are not, readers,' I told Helen, 'but they knew enough to know that Shakespeare was an entirely acceptable source of a name for their daughter. My mother had never read *The Two Gentlemen of Verona*, but at school she'd been made to learn by rote, and came to love, Shakespeare's tribute to his heroine:

Who is Silvia? What is she,
That all our swains commend her?
Holy, fair and wise is she;
The heaven such grace did lend her,
That she might admired be.

My mother liked this verse for its elegance, metrical regularity and felicitous use of rhyme. In fact, she dabbled in this kind of poetry, tried writing it herself, but it seemed the sense was often sacrificed to the sound.'

'I admire your mother's poetic aspirations, Sil, but "Holy, fair and wise?" Holy cow! What a dreadful legacy, you poor girl!' Helen repudiated, in exclamatory mode, this idealised Elizabethan version of the feminine to which I'd been consigned. 'Much better to be Sylvia Plath!" she declared. 'You know: vituperative and spiky, turning and burning; shrieks and slaying of vampire men.'

This reference to another Sylvia was hardly surprising, for we were at that time, and for some time after, compelled by the murderous lacerations of Plath. Feminism was in the air, it was standard undergraduate fare, and we breathed it all in—all that passionate rejection of tyrannical fathers, of cruel and faithless lovers. We too wanted to drive stakes into the hearts of brutal men.

I was right in guessing that my friend had been named after Helen of Troy. She told me that she was not, apparently, a pretty baby, but that her mother (a local society belle of legendary beauty) held out great hopes for her, determined that her daughter should become the face that launched an impressive number of upwardly mobile ships. As it turned out, the awkwardly coltish girl did indeed grow into a stunning adolescent, a veritable romantic cliché who turned many heads and broke countless hearts. And yet Helen was the least vain woman I have ever met. Utterly indifferent to clothes and hairstyles, to the usual bejewelled and spangled accessories of teenage girls, she was more at home in the library than the manicure parlour to which her mother insisted on sending her for a monthly polish and buff.

'Helen of Troy, indeed! How fatuously self-aggrandising, how stupidly self-mythologising!' she snorted. 'I've just been reading something by another Helen—an Australian, lord bless us. She writes like a dream—oblique and elliptical, linguistically poised and rhythmically deft, often about the emotional dead-ends of young women's lives. But her characters are utterly without self-pity and her style is bracing, witty and sharp. I've just finished reading one of her stories, Sil, about female friendship, which opens with two young women walking in—of all places—a cemetery, reading the tombstones, and it... Here, I'll read it to you....' as she fished out a book from her bag:

> '...my friend pointed to a headstone which said, *She lived only for others*. "Poor thing," said my friend. "On *my* grave I want you to write, *She lived only for herself*."

Self-sacrificing servitude, be damned!' Helen ended with a theatrical gesture to the heavens. And then we laughed together, sisters in defiance of propriety and rectitude, of saying and doing *the right thing*.

The subject of epitaphs came up again much later, at that stage in life when older relatives and, more problematically, parents die. When it becomes more difficult to make a joke. I had been to my mother's funeral two days earlier and made a point of meeting up with Helen, who, as it turned out, had been visiting an old friend who was dying. So death was in the air, and we needed to talk. As I began, falteringly, to construct a melancholy narrative about my mother's funeral, I realised that I'd been particularly upset by the eulogy. The speaker—the local priest—had known my mother for years and had been entrusted by her with the public summation of her life.

'Helen, his speech was so—so, impersonal, so generic and shockingly banal. I wanted to cry, or cry out, that it was all wrong. Oh yes, he talked about her good deeds and her courtesy and her work on the Hospital Board, but there was no sense of her *buried life*. He began by describing her as *a dutiful wife and caring mother*, and it kept getting worse. *Her long battle with illness/uncomplaining to the last/an exemplary life/sadly missed by all*. What a miserable end. Even Dad leaned over to me and whispered, *He does go on a bit.*'

Helen patted my hand and smiled a little wanly. She knew that I'd never been close to my mother but understood why I was offended by such impoverished prose.

'Let us make a pact,' she said quietly but decisively. 'Let us promise, my friend, to write one another's eulogies.'

She said it seriously, but it was impossible not to laugh, at least a little.

We continue to catch up, often, with late-night phone conversations—newsy, prolonged and almost always literary exchanges. (In our younger days, our husbands wondered *how on earth you find so much to talk about*). Sometimes we ring back the very next day for further ruminations, questions or advice. Our talk can be amusing or uplifting, even discomforting, but it is never uninteresting. My friend is intelligent, eloquent and widely read and I love her for her knowledge and perspicacity, for the way she always has a literary or scholarly reference to illuminate or amplify personal experience—mine, hers, that of family and friends.

I remember one particular conversation about a spell of illness—a bout of decidedly unpoetic gastroenteritis that, after a few days, had left me feeling pleasantly light-headed and disembodied. My words, floaty and inarticulate, drifted down the phone to my friend:

'It's so weird, Helen, this feeling, like being outside your body and totally unconcerned with all the things we usually worry about. And time is suspended, sort of arbitrary. I feel incredibly—*free*. Does that make sense?'

And Helen replied:

'Of course it does, Sil, I know just what you mean. It's a strange and rather beautiful kind of stasis, isn't it, where you feel you're at the still point of the turning world. Actually, now that you tell me this, I remember a remarkable piece of writing about your experience. One of Virginia Woolf's essays—*On Being Ill*, it's called. Yes, I know it's a disappointingly predictable title, but it's actually a nod to Romantic essayists like Hazlitt and De Quincy, who aimed for a kind of looseness and associativeness in their writing—rather like the state of mind which accompanies a fever or the flu. Anyway, there's a particular passage I remember...Hold on, I'll just get my copy...'

And she was off, searching hurriedly among her bookshelves, not wanting to lose the moment, the opportunity to share. I heard her on the end of the phone scrabbling through the pages, and her voice came back to me, full of excitement at the words:

' " I am in bed with influenza" – but what does that convey of the great experience; how the world has changed its shape; the tools of business grown remote; the sounds of festival become romantic like a merry-go-round heard across far fields; and friends have changed, some putting on a strange beauty, others deformed to the squatness of toads, while the whole landscape of life lies remote and fair, like the shore seen from a ship far out to sea...

That's brilliant, isn't it, that understanding of how illness can distort our perceptions. Friends "deformed to the squatness of toads" is particularly memorable. You can hear Woolf's revulsion for those she normally loves, transformed into these comic-grotesque amphibians. On the other hand, there's her sense of being utterly detached from life, the solidity and substantiality of the "real" world melting into air...The drift to death, perhaps. You must read it, Sil. I'll bring the book round in the morning.'

That was, and is, so like my friend, so like Helen, to move from the particular and personal to a philosophical and literary disquisition on the value of words. Such responses—which over the years I have come to call Hellenic—are never a sign of indifference to the other. There is nothing reductive, distanced or bloodlessly theoretical about her passionate textualising of life. It is experience intensified and enriched because more fully understood. Helen's knowledge is a gift, extended in the spirit of loving-kindness for which I love her, this especial and particular friend.

Some years earlier I'd lapsed into a very different kind of illness—protracted, mysterious and increasingly bizarre. For weeks I'd been unable to sleep. I began to feel headachy, knotted up and vaguely afraid, and, finally, unable to eat. I had no idea of what was happening to me. I'd always been a sound sleeper and a hearty eater; but now I felt blurred with insomnia and as if my flesh was melting away. I was turning into bone. The doctor told me to take some vitamins, prescribed sleeping pills and suggested I had too much time on my hands. I began to hear buzzing, mumbling conversations in my head and to see shadowy, misshapen figures flitting past my study window. I became certain I was dying of some rare disease and consulted medical books for answers, searching my face every day in the mirror for the red marks in the shape of a butterfly that would tell me my illness was real. The voices in my head became more insistent. I had no words to make sense of such bodily assailment. When I became convinced that my husband was trying to poison me because he tried to make me eat, we both knew it was time to *do something*. In hospital I heard the devil telling me I was an evil person who deserved to die. I looked at the pages of magazines I was unable to read and saw the faces, monstrously swollen and malevolent, of celebrities and models, glaring out at me. I learnt an entirely new lexicon. Doctors gave me words like *somatic delusions*, *psychotic episodes*, *clinical depression*—words at once alien, terrifying and strangely consoling.

Helen visited me every day, in my fearful, vertiginous and lonely space. Most of my memories are clouded and, perhaps, mercifully irretrievable. But I remember her presence and the way she would sit for hours on the hospital bed, holding my hand and talking with me. I told her about the tree outside my window. *I like to look at it*, I said. *Its branches are comforting.* On another, much darker day, when I could barely keep from weeping, I recalled for my friend the Shakespearean song that had given me my name:

'My mother's wish for me,' I sobbed in Helen's arms. 'But I have no wisdom, no grace; there is nothing to admire. I am woefully misnamed.'

Helen was lost for words. What could she say in the face of such misery, such dismal self-abasement? I thought we would never speak of it again. But next morning she brought in a yellowing copy of her Shakespeare, and read out to me the remaining stanzas of the song:

Is she as kind as she is fair?

> For beauty lives with kindness.
> Love doth to her eyes repair,
> To help him of his blindness,
> And, being helped, inhabits there.
>
> Then to Silvia let us sing,
> That Silvia is excelling;
> She excels each mortal thing
> Upon the dull earth dwelling.
> To her let us garlands bring.

My friend looked up from the page. 'I'd forgotten the rest of the verse,' she said, 'and indeed the play in its entirety. I read it last night for the first time in many years and was reminded that Silvia rejects this hyperbolic ode and the *subtle, perjured, false, disloyal man* who commands that it be sung.' Her voice was gentle but insistent. 'For the play which immortalises her is a testament to her intelligent, spirited and resourceful nature, her precious moral substance. I'd forgotten, Sil, that she defies the three most powerful men in the play, and'—she handed me her book—'that above all she is the kindest, most loyal of friends.'

I was both touched by such assiduous re-reading and deeply moved by Helen's loving reclamation of my name, my self. I knew in that moment that I would be well, that all would be well. And when I added, 'The repetition in the final stanza of Silvia's name is particularly gratifying', we smiled at one another in shared relief.

Helen wrapped her arms around me and then drew back, her hands on my shoulders. 'And tomorrow,' she said, 'I'll remember to bring the garlands.'

I have a recurring dream about my friendship with Helen. It is entirely and risibly transparent. In this dream I die. The details vary, but my death is always shockingly unexpected. Sometimes it's a car accident, driving home from a late-night jazz concert on a dark and corrugated road. It's raining—the sound of thunderous drumming fills the night—and the car skids into a tree and turns over and over and over. Or there is a rare and ravaging illness; I lapse into unconsciousness; there are frantic friends and doctors rushing about. In another dream there is a burning house, in which monstrous orange flames eat up the sky and my stricken face looks out through a window. In each variation, Helen is asked to speak at my funeral. The dreams never tell me what she said, but I know it is celebratory, not melancholy: I hear her words affirm my life. I've told my friend about these dreams and although she is, understandably, a little perturbed, she's also able to laugh when I tell her,

'I hope it *is* me first, Helen. I want you to compose and deliver that speech. You'll know precisely what to say.'

'Ah, my friend,' says Helen, 'is precision what you really want?' and I smile, knowing just what she means.

A voice in the dark

We stand looking down on his body. The chest is hairless and bony, the arms conspicuously thin, the hands folded decorously on the starchy whiteness of the hospital sheet. The familiar nose and chin, pointed like mine, now look oddly unfamiliar. His mouth is open, slack, obscenely lolling. It is the mouth above all which appalls me. They close the *eyes*, don't they, in deference to the dead and to those who look upon them? Why then leave this *mouth* agape, the careless revelation of an old man's toothless indignity? The body is utterly still. No gently rhythmic rise and fall of the chest, no sudden twitch of a hand. This is negation, not rest. The curtain drawn around the bed protects us from discreetly curious eyes, but fails to shut out the drone further down the ward of a radio sports commentary, the hum of patients' conversations, the clicking of briskly purposive heels on hospital tiles. It all goes on, wrongly.

My mother puts her hand on my father's cheek and strokes it softly back and forth, crooning, *No more pain, my darling. Now you are at peace.* Over the past month, she has seen him wither from a stout and hearty man, exhausted by insomnia and unrelenting pain. She told me he took so many painkillers that *he drooped over his meals; sometimes he even fell asleep. In the dark hours of the night he would call out my name, like a child.* My mother had tended him, day and night, herself unbearably tired and unable to sleep. It was a relief when my father finally went into hospital for his operation.

In the corridor, a nurse tells us that she will miss him too. *A lovely gentleman*, she says, *so charming and polite.* I thank her as I take the large plastic bag containing his clothes, wallet and a magazine, and walk with my mother in silence to the car. Driving home, I turn to see my mother's face red with anger, her eyes fixed straight ahead. Her voice spits, her vehemence is shocking: *Charming, my eye. Always charming to strangers, especially when he wanted something. They didn't have to live with him.*

Over the next few weeks I become a witness to my mother's relentless anger. Refusing to say what's supposed to be said, she pours forth, more to herself than to me, stories of disappointment and humiliation, of minor cruelties and more savage abasements. *He would follow me as I swept the kitchen floor*, she says, *pointing at crumbs I hadn't noticed. He shouted at me if dinner wasn't ready on time. He called me stupid in front of our friends, what would* you *know, he said. He never touched me except when he wanted sex.* She tells me about the time he brought her home from hospital, after her hysterectomy, when he'd yelled at her for jamming her seat belt in the door of the car. There, in the driveway, in front of the neighbours, he'd abused her as she struggled with her suitcase and her shame. Of course he was angry with her, angry for leaving him alone to cook for himself, fussing and fuming over domestic gadgets and machines that refused to work. One of the neighbours had been so disgusted by his behaviour that she refused to speak to him again. She told my mother later, *I just can't forgive him.*

There are other stories, similarly contemptible. There was the time, years ago, when he ordered his wife to wear two petticoats under her semi-transparent summer dresses. Or when he—a travelling salesman—cancelled the milk delivery because he suspected her of having an affair with the milkman. It was a story only rescued from risible cliché by the ferocious persistence of my father's accusations. He told my mother how to vote. At the dinner table he would demand the salt, second helpings, complain about the fatty meat, gesturing imperiously, eating noisily, a boor as well as a bully. After his retrenchment, he restricted my mother to one outing a week to the city with a friend. He would wait on the front steps until she came home. Suspiciously superintending, he would always insist on knowing what she'd done, how much she'd spent.

In the weeks following my father's death, I help my mother tie up financial matters—finalising the will, notifying the relevant government agencies, closing bank accounts. He has left nothing. Even worse, we discover large debts on his credit card, money taken out to bet, and lose, on the horses. We've known about his gambling for years, but the size of the debt shocks both of us, and enrages my mother. She tells me, *A wife can put up with so many things, but when the husband can't even be a good provider...What kind of a man is that?*

On one of our various trips to the city, we stop in front of a florist's shop, silenced in mid-conversation by a window full of bright yellow blooms, scarlet bunches abundant and lavish. My mother says, deliberatively, *You know, he never once gave me flowers.* And there, in the noisy street, bodies brushing past us with busy intent, she is motionless and crying. I stroke my mother's arm, thinking, she cannot, surely, mean *never*.

The last time I saw my father alive was the day before his death. Waiting for his operation, he'd seemed uncharacteristically self-effacing, even serene. At the end of the visit he'd accompanied me to the door of his hospital room. Shuffling with obvious difficulty, he'd played the part of the courtly European gentleman, thanking me for coming, his voice surprisingly gentle. I was disconcerted by such graciousness and by the apparent possibility of transformation in the face of suffering. Later I learnt it was the morphine he'd been given for the pain.

The night after his death, family members meet to compose a newspaper obituary and a speech for the funeral. My brother Karl, always methodical and decisive, has taken charge—the well-meaning orchestrator of the required sentiments. He keeps prompting our mother for complimentary and consoling words about her husband, our father. She offers merely perfunctory remarks and indifferent shrugs of the shoulder. At the end of an hour, Karl is able to note only that our father had been an affable, joke-telling salesman who liked to debate current affairs and who amused the neighbours with his loud barracking of the football on TV. I see my brother's agitation as he takes me aside and asks, quietly, what's going on. *Good God*, he declares, *a man's life has to be worth something. There has to be more to say.* I am very fond of my brother but am unable, and perhaps unwilling, to console. *You have to understand*, I say, trying not to patronise, *how difficult it's been for her all these years. She isn't sorry that he's dead.* It's the closest I come to feeling sorry for my father. Later that night Karl asks me to help deliver the eulogy, but I am frozen by a terrifying sense of having nothing to say. At the funeral, my brother makes a speech which is amusingly anecdotal and which earns him praise from those few in attendance. I understand that his words are for our mother's sake and for the sake of appearances, and I am grateful.

Thinking back now, over the past few days, I find myself wondering about my father's body. Watching it, I'd been alarmed by its bewildering conjunction of presence and absence. Persistently corporeal and yet utterly still, this body seemed to me neither dead nor alive. But now that his body has gone, has been lost to me, I feel very little about the fact of his death and almost nothing for the man himself. Like my mother, I can't pretend to have loved him. I'm unable even to respect him. I knew him as a man for whom value was always a matter of dollars and cents. I remember the year he voted for the political party that, after days of careful calculation, he estimated would give him five dollars more than the other. As someone who thought his cleverness vindicated by bogus insurance claims. Who often asked me how much I earned but never once about the intangible profits of my work as a teacher. Whatever sadness I feel, then, is for my mother, my brother and myself, as we grieve for the husband and the father we never had.

My friends have told me and I know from many books about the perplexing ambiguities and unpredictability of grief—how it can strike you unawares, out of the blue. But I'd never expected to feel sorry about my father's death; indeed, a year after the event, it almost feels like he'd never lived at all. But now I find myself becoming conscious, if only from a nagging sense of filial duty, to consider my father's side of the story. Was it all bluster and bullying, petty selfishness and self-pity? Am I so unmoved, so unmovable, that I'm unable to conjure up some moments, any moment, which might represent that monstrous ego in a kindlier light? I recall, reluctantly, the two occasions on which I'd seen my father cry. I'd come across him in the living room, where he was reading a magazine, wiping streams of tears from his face. I was twelve years old, and vaguely unnerved by this strange spectacle, this unmanning of the bully of my childhood. He looked up and blushed and, in faltering half-sentences, explained that he had just finished reading a story about the death of a family pet. It was a St Bernard, he told me, just like the one he'd had as a child in snowy Europe. A dog, it would seem, of lovable largeness and tongue-slurping devotion, which accompanied him daily on family errands, was known to everyone in the neighbourhood, was patted, fussed over and mourned for years after he died. I noted that the magazine on my father's lap was *The Reader's Digest*, and, already the literary snob, I registered silent contempt for the sentimentality of both the text and the reader. So young, and so stony-hearted.

I recall a second scene of exposure. I was alone in the kitchen with my father. He told me that my mother had gone to the country for a few days, to stay with a friend. I was fifteen, and acutely conscious not only of the loud argument the night before—voices sharp and bitter, denouncing and angry, behind my parents' bedroom door—but also of the many silences, the glowering faces and stubborn withdrawals, all the corrosive markers of marital estrangement. My father was pacing the room and running his hands through his thick white hair. *She says she's fed up*, he said, more to himself than to me. *She says she may never come back*. He stopped and looked at me directly and I saw that his eyes were full of tears. *You know*, he said, *in all these years, she never once came to me*. I was both stranded by adolescent embarrassment and strangely touched by his old-fashioned turn of phrase. She never, in modern parlance, initiated sex. She never showed him that she wanted him, made him feel desired, desirable. The moment passed and my father left the room.

49

There are other memories, fugitive and incomplete. Half-recalled half-sentences, an image, a gesture, which offer some dimly apprehended sense of paternal pride or affection. I remember my father, drenched with rain, standing on the sidelines of a hockey field, yelling encouragement to his unathletic daughter. *C'mon, Maria, tackle, tackle her!* he shouted, waving his ineffectual umbrella. There was a compliment for my school ball gown, a beaming face at my wedding as he walked me down the aisle, an awkward cradling of his first grandchild. But these fragments fail to move me. They seem to me, after all, the unexceptional memories of conventional female milestones, in which my father merely performed a series of unexceptional and conventional roles.

There is a more intensely realised memory of an outing in the country on one of his travelling salesman's trips, in which I sat proudly beside him in the front seat of his brand-new car. Even now, thirty years on, the sharp smell of vinyl evokes for me that special day, me and my dad driving on long country roads, the red dust whipping up around us, farm gates being opened, dogs running alongside the car, a lime-flavoured ice cream at the end of the journey as a reward for my patience. And there was my graduation day when my father, round and replete with pride, boasted of his prize-winning daughter to some bemused dignitaries. *Maria's going overseas to a top-class university*, he told them several times. Besuited and slightly tipsy, embarrassing and endearing, he hugged my mother jubilantly and waved his wine glass in the air.

But now, after all these years, after his death, I mostly recall his arrogance, his anger, his indifference to those who might have loved him. I remember the hour before his return from work, which my mother and I would savour before the arrival of those demands, complaints, criticisms, that drove us away. The afternoon teas with friends, when my mother's social pleasantries were derided, shouted down. Proclaiming his opinions, banging his fist on the table. All that noise, the fury and the tedium of it, his inability ever to pause, to listen.

I am left with a final memory of my father, a story my mother told me some months after his death. An unexpected and perplexing coda. It seems that on the night before his operation, he'd phoned an old acquaintance—someone he hadn't seen in fifteen years—to say that he wasn't going to make it. My father had no close friends. Like so many men of his generation, all his emotional connections had been forged and sustained by his wife. And unlike my mother, he'd lost contact with the Europe of his youth. I knew from my father's boasting of the existence of older and successful siblings: a doctor, a lawyer and a priest—a professional triumvirate whose ghostly presence he would sometimes invoke as proof of his intellectual superiority, and to lament the wealth that might have been. He hadn't corresponded with them since leaving his homeland. He didn't know what had become of them, whether they were even alive.

Years later, an old man in an altogether different country, he'd chosen to call a virtual stranger, late at night from the payphone in the cold and silent hospital corridor, given his name, exchanged greetings and said he knew he was going to die. In barely a whisper. Out of the blue. The bewildered acquaintance had asked a few questions, found a context and pieced together a medical history of sorts. He remembered offering some garbled sympathy and a rather forced pep talk, and the conversation, such as it was, trailing off into uneasy silence. And of course my father's dismal prediction was right. He didn't make it. After months of massive doses of painkillers, his kidneys were barely functional. His heart, already weakened by years of angina, simply gave up.

When my mother was finally told this story, she was both puzzled and upset. Why had her husband called this man in the middle of the night? Someone he hadn't seen, hadn't spoken to, for so many years. Why hadn't he called his wife, as he'd always done before? In the face of such terrible questions, I can offer only platitudes. *Sometimes it's easier to talk to strangers*, I try to explain. *Perhaps he didn't want to worry you. Or perhaps he was simply confused.*

Today I'm driving home from work along the river, listening to the radio. It's one of those balmy days in Perth, in May: the warm sun streaming through the car window, an afternoon breeze gently scudding the water, the white sails of yachts puffed out proudly against an impossibly clear blue sky. The voice on the radio is familiar, the voice of a former broadcaster and interviewer, now being interviewed herself about her professional and personal life. She's recalling one of her old programs, which had featured many high-profile public achievers speaking about, still grappling with, their search for meaning. Over the years she had talked with academics and intellectuals, political activists, business people, artists; even a vacuous socialite who was surprisingly articulate and emotionally astute. I register fragments of conversation as the woman now speaks about her own search for meaning: her former marriage, her childlessness, her religious conversion; the difficulties of solitariness and the pleasures of solitude. I am lulled, as always, by her voice. It has a calmness, a sense of conviction without complacency, of unassertive faith, perhaps. She sounds like a woman whose serenity has been earned.

And then, as the program comes to an end, she is asked, finally, how she would like to be remembered after her death. As I drive along the river, feeling the warmth of the sun, I see the sails of the yachts and the blue of the sky, and I know in my heart what she will say. *As someone who loved...and was loved.* I wonder, for a moment, whether her pause is merely a rhetorical trick, one of the skills of a public performer aiming for emotional effect. But the sentiment sounds real enough. This, I feel, is the voice of someone who knows herself to be blessed, who pauses to give silent thanks for the gift of loving and being loved. And suddenly, unexpectedly, I think of my father, calling from the hospital phone, alone and whispering. I see his face, pale and bony, his frail hands barely able to move the dial, his thin legs beneath his checked dressing gown. Did he feel himself to be someone unloving and unloved? Did he know himself to be, on that last night, finally and fearfully, unblessed? And because I see him there so clearly, because I will never know the answer, will never know if that was after all his real question, I find myself at last able to cry.

Somewhere else

That night, after the rush of the children's mealtime-bathtime-sleeptime, they flopped down as they often did in front of the TV. An hour or so of mindless viewing was about all they were good for. Two relentlessly rambunctious boys, neither of them sound sleepers, was enough to reduce both parents to vegetative and mirthless silence, as splices of chat shows, cop shows, game shows and ads flicked past in stupefying succession. Tonight the fare was more than usually dispiriting: reality shows on every commercial channel, and tired re-runs of tired sitcoms on pay TV. Paul skimmed the guide to find something remotely watchable.

'Oh, here's a good one,' he grumbled sarcastically. 'Female infanticide—just the right nightcap after an exhausting day.'

Clara was offended by such flippancy and was prepared to tell him so.

'That's a bit rough, Paul. It's not something to make fun of, you know. It's a serious issue, a matter of grave injustice.'

'Course it is, hon. Don't get on your moral high horse. We already know this appalling stuff. And anyway, it's happening somewhere else, in places where we have no influence.' He yawned, his rather showy—what Clara sometimes thought of as his *look-at-me-aren't-I-a-devoted-father*—kind of yawn. 'I'm off to bed before the boys wake up.'

Clara caught the remote control as he casually flung it aside and didn't bother to say goodnight. 'Damn you,' she said, a little more loudly than she'd intended, as she switched to the multicultural channel. The program had already started and immediately she remembered watching it some time ago, not long after Robbie was born. Did this mean that nothing had changed? There were the vaguely familiar faces of politicians and academics in a series of earnest interviews with rows of books lined up behind them, the interviewer's sympathetic nods, shots of barren landscapes, remote villages, and the bizarre conjunction of squalor and peasant women attired in gorgeously coloured robes. And all those statistics and stories, all the ghastly practices in those places where female babies are unwanted, an economic burden, who are killed or left to die. Clara winced as she heard, once again, the details. Smothered with wet towels, strangled or allowed to starve. Or forced to eat dry, unhulled rice that punctured their windpipes. Made to swallow poisonous powdered fertiliser. Across the ocean; barely imaginable. Paul was right: she already knew these stories, the horror of specificity, narrated here in the modulated tones of a well-known western female voice. *That voice*, Clara found herself muttering for the second time; it was so poised, so expressive, so irritating. No, more than irritating—so wrong: one of those *listen-to-me-being-so-sensitive-and-caring* kinds of voices. She wanted to slap the speaker, tell her to shut up. *You're being stupid, Clara*, she heard herself saying. *Go to bed.*

It was the usual disturbed night, with both David and Robbie waking several times, demanding a drink, the toilet or a cuddle. *How come other people's kids sleep through the night?*

Paul complained after a second waking. (To his credit, Clara acknowledged, he did his fair share of tending to the needs of these night-time tyrants, even more so now that Clara was gearing up for returning to work.) *Five and two years old, and they're still behaving like babies!* he sighed, slumping into bed. No wonder he hadn't wanted another one, Clara thought. She still remembered how she'd tried to talk him into having one last baby. She'd begun with rational arguments: there was still plenty of time, she'd told him, she was only thirty-five, she was healthy; her job would be waiting for her. And there was a weight of evidence—she flourished the learned article she'd been reading—to suggest that a third child made for better-balanced children all round. When Paul demurred, she'd changed tack, tried cajoling and teasing. *Paul, I promise you, you won't have to lift a finger,* she'd pleaded. *I'll be the perfect Stepford wife.* She flirted with him, bought the sexiest lingerie she'd owned in years, she'd cooked him gourmet meals. *I'll do anything for you,* she sang to him, like Oliver, all innocent-eyed and appealing. *Wouldn't it be nice,* she said as she nuzzled his neck, *to try for a girl?* When he'd maintained his resistance, she even briefly toyed with the idea of forgetting her contraception, but she knew this wasn't right. A baby should belong to both of them, and she didn't want any child of hers, of theirs, to be the product of deception. In the end, financial constraints and Paul's reasoning—his talk of broken nights and fractious days—had prevailed. But now, as her husband turned out the light, Clara plumped up her pillow crossly and turned over on her side.

The next morning it was business as usual. How was it her boys could be so high-jinxed and jumping, when she, still in her coffee-stained chenille at ten a.m., could barely lift her toast?

Nevertheless, she'd promised them an expedition to the city, an afternoon, as it turned out, of high hilarity, fuelled by the latest Disney animation at the Multiplex and—stupidly—the rare treat of glimmeringly greasy junk food. David was flying along the footpath, making machine-gun noises, arms outstretched and occasionally, just to scare his mother, veering perilously close to the kerb. His brother, fretful with exhaustion, additives and preservatives, was squalling querulously. His tiny feet beat beat beat on the seat of his pusher, demanding release; his fists were squashed red balls of rage. Clara saw, thankfully, that relief was in sight, their house only a block away, and she sighed as she told herself, *No more laddish outings these holidays, you fool*. And it was then that the strange thing happened. The street looked different, just like that, as if she were suddenly walking onto a deserted movie set, all hyperrealist clarity and preternatural silence. It was the trees she saw first. They were lopped, every one of them, their tops flattened as if by some crazed topiarian. They lined both sides of the road like so many extraterrestrial spacecraft, spookily hovering over the spread of clipped front lawns. Then Clara noticed the rubbish bins, one for every front verge, standing like dark green sentinels, grim and immovable, their jaws shut tight. Dozens of them in serried ranks. As if lying in wait.

She shook herself. Isn't this what you did to snap yourself back to the real world? Shaking herself did a lot of good, she knew. It was her mother's cure for childhood daydreaming or dawdling: *Shake yourself up, Clara*, she would say; or, *Shake a leg. You have to stop being silly*, she would add in moments of exasperation. *You have to get moving. It gets the blood flowing.* And it helped, it always did. And so Clara took a deep breath and started walking again—it was only then she realised she'd been standing still—and again she registered the giddy run of her five-year-old as he reached the front garden of their house. Robbie was still screeching and banging with his feet; everything was returning to normal. By the time Clara caught up with David at the front door, she was recomposed. She took the key from her purse and was relieved by how easily it fitted into the lock. Door open. Home.

This incident was in itself no cause for concern. In fact, to prove this, to test herself, on the very next day Clara made herself look closely at those flat-topped trees. They were odd, yes, even a little sad, but perfectly intelligible—the result, no doubt, of budget cuts and council-worker haste. And when rubbish collection came round, the ominous guards of the day before were nowhere in sight. They were merely large green plastic receptacles—familiar, convenient, efficient. It was all reassuringly real.

But less than a week later something else happened. Fleeting, like the distorted vision of the street, but, Clara had to acknowledge, more disconcerting. She and the boys were standing at a set of traffic lights, waiting for the *Jolly Green Man*, as David called the Walk sign. She was attending carefully to her children, as she always did in such situations, holding the fidgety David's hand and carrying Robbie on her hip. The pedestrian light came on and David started to jerk forward, but Clara stood still, holding him back. She heard him urge her on: *Come on, Mamma, the Jolly Green Man's here*; but she knew they had to wait for someone else standing behind them. Who was it? Clara turned to look but there was no one there. She thought there'd been someone, sure there was a body; she could sense a shape, a presence; she could even smell it, a sweet, flowery fragrance. But there was nothing there, nothing but a space. And then she heard her older boy whining with annoyed incomprehension, *Come on, Mamma, what are you waiting for?* By the time Clara came to her senses the light had turned red and she had no choice but to respond to her irritated son. *Sorry, Petal, I was daydreaming.*

It wasn't until late that evening that Clara had the luxury of thinking about what this might mean. What had happened today, she knew, was of a different order, altogether more troubling, than those trees and bins. That earlier lapse was surely the result of tiredness and a spot of dehydration after a day in the city with her two rollicking boys. Simple physiology; cause and effect. But today she hadn't been tired or hungry or thirsty; she was only just starting out on their morning walk to the park. So what did she think was there, behind her? What or who was she waiting for? And actually to *smell* someone? This hallucinatory moment—for Clara knew it as such—was beginning to unnerve her, hours after the event. She found herself looking at the doorway of the TV room, trying not to wonder if there was someone behind it, and then thinking, *This is a little crazy.*

She made a conscious decision not to speak of this, any of this, to anyone. Oh she knew that Paul would listen sympathetically, but the wry grin would also be there, that skeptical, faintly arrogant look he sometimes shot in her direction. Nor could she relate these incidents, these—oddities—to her friends, rational beings every one of them, who rejected intimations of otherworldliness, visitations, hallucinations, presentiments of the unknown. They would, surely, laugh and tell her that she needed more sleep. So things were not said; and what was not said, particularly when there was so much to be done—feeding, cleaning, cooking, playing, shopping, feeding again—began to be erased, began not to have happened at all. It wasn't, in the end, too difficult.

And then the dreams began. Clara was a daydreamer, yes, but not a nightdreamer; or, more to the point, she recalled little or nothing at all of her nocturnal psychic life. This, Paul had joked more than once, was *evidence of a highly repressed personality*; and she'd retorted, all defensive pomposity, that dreams were *in all likelihood nothing but the neurological detritus of the preceding day's events*. And yet here she was, confronted by so many of them, night after night, her bewildered night-time self rolling and rolling down a high steep hill, her limbs flailing, unable to stop. Insistent dreams, tormenting dreams, dreams of such vivid particularity, such visceral intensity, that waking life the next day seemed paradoxically and strangely unreal. Dreams about babies. In the first one Clara saw an infant in the distance, lying naked and pitiable, in a blasted field. She ran towards her, longing to wrap her up in the warmth of a deep blue shawl, but just as she was about to scoop her up, the baby disappeared—simply melted into the air. The next night Clara dreamed she was sitting with a baby in a field of flowers: swathes of purple crocuses, irises and hyacinths. The tiny infant was wearing a frilly dress, beautifully herringboned across the bodice and embroidered with daisies. Needlework of loving intricacy. Clara was singing to this rosy bud of a baby, a song about Peter Rabbit with a fly upon his nose, when the sky turned deadly black, there was a trembling rumbling sound and the earth opened up in front of them. Before she could move, Clara saw the hole in the ground spread, like a yawning monster rising from sleep, and she saw the baby holding out her chubby arms in terror as the earth, simply and dreadfully, swallowed her up. Clara was frozen. She saw the flowers wilt in a fast fade-out; she saw all the trees wither and die.

The most disturbing dream came to her two nights later. It was located in what must have been a hospital—all silver instruments and gleaming white walls, bright lights, flashing monitors. Another movie-set, it seemed. The room smelled of antiseptic and orderly efficiency. There were three women with muscular white arms and stony faces, dressed identically in starched white uniforms, leaning over her as she lay immobilised on a narrow bed ringed with metal bars. The women were pulling something out of her body, but Clara felt no sensation at all, not a thing. The procedure was short. She became aware of another presence in the room, another woman in white standing in the background. This woman had a dark face and dark hands, which she kept wringing, and there were tears, effortless tears, coursing down her face, spilling at her feet in an opalescent pool which flowed across the room and under the door. No one else noticed this weeping woman. When Clara woke from her dream, her face too was wet with tears.

Paul woke to find his wife curled up beside him, trembling. He touched her gently, his face puzzled, but before he could speak she posed him, posed herself, an impossible question:

'Paul. Do you think we brought the wrong baby home from the hospital?'

She could read the expression on his face. She had sense enough to register that he wasn't amused, and just enough sense to explain,

'I've been having dreams, about losing a baby. I think it was a girl.'

Paul laughed and patted her arm. 'I think they're called wish-fulfillment dreams. Those bloody kids are never going to sleep through the night.'

Over the next few weeks, Clara managed to make this thought, this crazy thought, go away, this idea that she had taken the wrong baby home. That Robbie wasn't hers, wasn't theirs. She couldn't stop it coming, but at least she was able to get rid of it, shoo it away like a blowfly, a dirty buzzing thing. The dreams, mercifully, stopped; but in a cruel and seemingly uncontrollable reversal of fate, Clara's daytime world took on the dark imaginings of the night. She looked at her child and failed to recognise him. This second son, who was as close to her as her own skin. Now she caught herself scrutinising his face intently, searching for a family resemblance—some likeness in the mouth or eyes, the shape of the chin—that wasn't there. When he ran away from her in a game of hide-and-seek, she screamed out for him, beside herself with fear until she found him. But when she saw him, his face was unfamiliar, as though her real child had been spirited away and replaced by this freckle-faced imposter. She began to peer openly at babies on television, in magazines, looking for the face she would know as soon as she saw her. She composed an ad for the personal section of the local paper: *Wanted: a baby girl. Probably has fair skin, fair hair and a pointed chin. Taken by mistake from the Camperdell Women's Hospital, on 19th April 2005.* When Grandma insisted that Robbie had his father's incredibly long fingers, and speculated on his stellar career as a concert pianist, Clara heard herself saying, so no one could hear, *I wish you'd shut up, I wish you'd just shut up.* Her stupid mother-in-law, she muttered; she had no idea.

How can one describe the undoing of a perfectly rational being? This strange and alarming unravelling of a self? Sometimes it takes a long time; it's so gradual, so insidiously slow, that there's never a point when you can say, yes, that's the moment, that's when she started to fall apart. At other times it happens very quickly, before anyone can see it coming. Clara was now in that peculiar and untenable state in which she knew she was becoming unhinged and yet was unable to stop herself. She could just catch a glimpse of a lunatic woman out of the corner of her eye and recognise her as herself. How frightening this was, and how utterly hilarious. She heard herself laughing. She knew that she was walking outside, alone, and sliding into the car, not knowing what she was going to do, only knowing that she needed to get out of the house, needed to go somewhere else, go anywhere.

That was how she found herself driving down to the shopping mall, the local emporium. She knew it would be full of people, the more the better, Clara thought, all the better to find her missing baby. The sliding doors of the mall opened for her, for her alone, effortlessly. Straightaway the noise rushed over her like a huge wave; the light was brilliant, dazzling, all molten rivers of orange and red. It was like walking into a burning building, where the flames leap up and lick you, draw round you with their roar and heat, but which you have to walk into all the same. All that vibrant colour, the incessant movement. Clara shielded her eyes from the flames and steeled herself, knowing that she must remain inconspicuous and calm. She mustn't make a sound, mustn't stare too long into the many prams and pushers that glided past her. One false step could prove her undoing. She felt a buzzing in her ears, a tom-tom throbbing in her head; she could see rows and rows of trumpeting colours, so many shops heaped with so many things, rubbish, it was all rubbish, she knew, lots of shiny stuff, baubles and bracelets and rings for noses, things which made a noise. She tried to block out the light and the din, the objects streaking past her behind walls of glass—spangled jewellery, shiny plates, a kaleidoscope of dummies dressed in swirling colours, silver machines lined up like rows of coffins. What looked like a large rabbit, blue and furry, grinned out at her from a window. What was she looking for? She would surely remember as soon as she saw it, wouldn't she? There were so many people moving about, zig-zagging and bumping and rushing, and some of them were pushing things, prams and strollers, all of them hung with mobiles and more shiny things for a baby who couldn't even see, more rubbish, just getting in the way. And all the babies were covered up so much it was impossible to see them, their bodies buried under mounds of blankets, pink, blue, and all kinds of frills and flounces, fancy lace. They looked like so many dead babies.

Clara gave up whatever she was looking for and sat down on a bench, spent and sick at heart from the flashing lights, the high-pitched scream of noises melting together, shrieks and spruikers and thumping music, thumping thumping, ceaselessly. She was rocking lightly, mechanically, back and forth, back and forth, in time to the music. How long had she been sitting on the bench? You couldn't sit there for too long, people might want to take your place or they might think you were very lazy or had something wrong with you. So she stood up and headed off, slowly, trying to think clearly and remind herself why she'd come here, what she was searching for. A sharp voice snapped at her, *Watch where you're going, lady*, and she smiled, stupidly. She must walk more carefully. She must just keep on walking, go somewhere. More people were bumping into her and then someone was steadying her by the elbow. A voice said, *Are you all right, Madam? Are you all right, Madam? Are you all right, Madam?* Clara mumbled with irritation, *Why does he keep saying the same thing to me, over and over again?* And then there was a noise behind her, a lot of rushing about and waving hands and open mouths, and then everything slowed down, became blurred and silent, and then there was nothing.

'The next thing she saw clearly, in sharp silhouette, was her husband's face. He was holding her hand and staring blankly out of a window, looking sad. So sad, all crumpled up. But then he turned to see her awake, her eyes shining, and he leaned over and kissed her tenderly on the forehead.

'Oh my love, my love,' was all he could say.

Clara didn't know where she was. She could see that the room was large, white, sparkling clean, and she could see her husband holding her hand, looking grave, taking care.

'I've been somewhere else, haven't I?' she said, and then she remembered. The lights, the noise, the strange objects, so many people, so many, so much, and a hollowness in the pit of her stomach. 'I was trying to find a baby.'

'What happened? Surely it's not all this business about...?' He trailed off, his tone both uncomprehending and pleading. 'Clara,' he continued, searching her face, 'we've all been so worried about you. When they called me from the hospital and I found you here, sobbing in your sleep...I thought my heart would break.'

Despite her exhaustion, Clara felt well enough to smile. She looked around her, at the clean white walls, the monitors, the half-open blinds. Her body sank down into the cool, smooth whiteness of the bedsheets; she began to give herself up to the quiet of the room, its soothing, enveloping calm. And then, unbidden, as if she were dreaming, she remembered the woman with the dark face, the dark hands which she kept wringing, the woman with the endless tears falling down, falling down. Clara felt, like a weight in her heart, all her good fortune: the love of her husband and children; the luxury of choice; the sheer accident of being who she was, where she was, and not somewhere else. There was no wrong baby. She and Paul would walk together through the hospital doors and drive through the comforting night to their home. Their boys would be sleeping, perhaps, their faces soft with dreams. Grandma would be watching over them, solicitous and proud, still marvelling at Robbie's long, exquisitely delicate fingers. And in the morning there would be breakfast—glasses of milk, honey on toast—and sticky smears on faces, sticky kisses to start the day. Through the tears that wouldn't stop, Clara could see everything so clearly: the bright silver toaster; the shining kitchen bench—black, with flecks of gold; the spruce white curtains dotted with sprigs of purple flowers. All this she had; so much, so gleaming and so achingly unreal.

Fitting in

Ester was a child in the fifties and of the fifties, taught by her parents to be polite, diligent and neat. The daughter of a salesman and a seamstress, she lived with them in the hot, dusty wheatbelt of Western Australia. Berdimup was a relatively large country town that the locals liked to describe as *hustling and bustling*. It had recently acquired a *delicatessen* and the picture theatre had started showing films starring women with sensually alliterative names, like Greta Garbo and Brigitte Bardot. But it was also in Berdimup that Ester learnt the real meaning of another word. *Mutti*. Anyone's mother in German, and her own very particular mother. She had other names as well, of course, but Mutti was what she called herself in the family and what Ester had always called her. It was precisely the right word for her. She was soft like the vowel and strong like the 't' in the middle, the mother who hugged and soothed and waited for Ester at the gate of their house every day after school, and the mother who sewed for long hours into the night and who never seemed to cry. Ester loved this coincidence, that a word could fit so happily with what it described. Lyrical and talismanic, *Mutti* was almost a poem in itself.

In her class at school Ester wore flounced nylon dresses and patent leather shoes like all the other ten-year-old girls. But she knew, without being told, that she wasn't quite the same as those other girls, who were freckled, rangy and sandy-haired, while she was smooth-skinned and dark-eyed and could recite many poems by heart. She had come with her parents from a faraway place, where, her mother told her, snow fell in pearly drifts and children wore huge woollen mittens and puffy anoraks. Ester liked to hear such stories. She especially liked the one about her mother as a child, her first memory of winter. *It was wunderbar!* Mutti exclaimed. *I remember standing outside, singing a Christmas carol. My face was tingling with happiness and my words streamed out in strands in the cold cold air.* Ester also knew that her family was different because they ate different food, salami and sauerkraut and thick slabs of bread spread with lard and sprinkled all over with bright red dots of paprika. And they ate differently as well—expansively, operatically, like the language they spoke to one another when no one else was listening.

It was important, Ester's parents had always told her, to mix with Australians. Despite the food, the table manners and the strange words, they were determined to fit in from the moment they saw the glittering coastline and the promise of so much dazzling light, the cloudless sky. DPs, they were called—Displaced Persons—soon to be re-named New Australians, as long as they worked hard, learnt to speak English and put up with the heat. There were, of course, adjustments to be made. As a young child, Ester remembered hearing for the first time the sounds of Australian birds, and Mutti puzzling over the squawks of the magpies and the mocking cacophony of the kookaburras. *Listen*, she said to her daughter, pointing to the trees, *they make noise, not music. Not like the nightingale, with its haunting song.*

There was also a new language to learn. It wasn't too difficult for Ester's father, whose schoolboy Latin enabled him to manage weighty abstractions such as *culpability* and *solicitude*. His first purchase after getting a job was a fat Webster's dictionary to expand his increasingly large vocabulary. Mutti, however, struggled with intransitive verbs and with prepositions that left her in danger of getting under, not onto, a bus. When the family moved to the country, Ester's father—recently reinvented as a hardware salesman—visited the cockies on their farms and soon learnt to lean over their fences, yarning in the requisite laconic style. But the local vernacular proved much trickier for Mutti. When she took quite literally the request to 'bring a plate', the women at the church social were polite enough to hide a smile. *These Australians*, Mutti had said a little smugly to Ester's father, *are they so poor they cannot afford their own china?*

Sunday School in Berdimup was an opportunity for Ester to mix with some of the neighbouring children. Her parents were not religious. Indeed, they spurned the idea of a superintending deity of any description, preferring instead to trust in hard work and a good education to get ahead. Nevertheless, they understood the importance of fitting in to the practices of the town's parishioners. *It is good for business*, Ester's father said, *to be seen putting a coin in the collection bowl and mouthing the hymns.* Ester liked the Sunday School teacher, whose wavy blonde hair and golden skin were illuminated, saint-like, by the sunlight streaming through the window, but she didn't understand why the boys and girls pinched and punched each other under the table when Miss Martin wasn't looking. Ester tried hard to learn her lessons. She was the only child in the group who could recite the whole of Psalm 23 without a stumble or mistake. This had been easy, since she was a clever, conscientious child and because she liked the sounds of the words when she said them—sonorous, majestic and vaguely comforting. A girl poked her tongue at Ester and a boy leaned over and hissed *Bitch* in her ear. It was a word she had heard in the school playground, a mean, slitted word that made her think of snakes or sharply jabbing knives. It was nicer to think of *green pastures* and *still waters* and *paths of righteousness*.

Ordinary school, too, was for Ester this odd mixture of pleasure and moments of minor and seemingly motiveless malignity. Her teachers were fond of her, praising the neatness and detail of her work and her extensive knowledge of matters mathematical, geographical and grammatical. There was Mr Gardiner, a ginger-haired barrel of a man, who would flourish the pages of Ester's exemplary homework as he walked around the classroom, cuffing the occasional sniggering boy behind the ears. Or the year after, the beautiful Miss Hanrahan, with her milky skin and silky voice, reading aloud Ester's poetry, then making a point about its *happy use of rhyme*. Even the sing-song *sotto voce* from the back of the classroom—*Happy crappy!*—couldn't diminish Ester's pleasure. She tried not to show it but couldn't stop the warm glow inside her spreading out to form a bright red flush all over her face.

In the playground the boys would sometimes run around her in circles and call her silly names, like *Krautface* and *Strudelbum*. Or they would tug at her dark wiry plait—braided carefully each morning by her Mutti—before they ran away, laughing loudly as they pretended to be magpies, spreading their arms in wider and wider circles, just before they swooped. Ester had grown used to this kind of larking. But on one particular day Rodney Jackson pulled her hair particularly hard. It hurt so much that Ester's head throbbed for the rest of the morning, a dull, persistent ache, accompanied by a strange sense that she had done something wrong, that *she* was to blame. Blame rhymed with shame, and somehow this word seemed to fit with the swirl of feelings in her stomach, feelings that stayed with her long after the throbbing in her head had died away.

It happened on one of those molten February days when even the hardiest of Australian schoolchildren begin to wilt and fret and grizzle about wanting to go home. Outside the classroom, the bitumen playground shimmered and swooned, melting into a black and deadly lake. Inside, heads drooped, bodies slumped and fat flies droned lethargically, their legs stuck to the windowpanes. Even the hands of the clock seemed immobilised. Only Vivienne Carter and Lorraine Best rallied themselves, declaring that they should be allowed to leave when the temperature reached 100 degrees. *There's a rule, Sir!* they proclaimed, and, *'Snot fair!* They were big, bossy girls, champion swimmers both of them, with blonde straggly hair bleached green by the chlorine in the local pool. Rosy-faced with perspiration, indeed wet all over, Ester was inclined to agree with them, but she remembered that Mutti had always told her never to complain about the heat. She kept her mind on the teacher's task, filling out the worksheet on capital cities of the world. Occasionally she looked up to see a child or two glaring at her, as though she was responsible for this sticky incarceration. At last the bell went and, without waiting to be dismissed, thirty-two children, mysteriously revitalised, grabbed their bags and scrambled to the door, jostling, pushing, hollering in jubilation. Ester waited until she was the only one left in the room and, barely able to lift herself up from the seat, she peeled her nylon dress away from her legs and slipped out in silent relief.

She made her way home, as always, by walking on the big pipeline that her father had told her ran all the way to a faraway place called Kalgoorlie. *A marvellous feat of Australian engineering!* he had exclaimed. *It brings the gift of water to many thousands of people in this dry dry land.* Now, despite the heat, Ester enjoyed balancing on this enormous cylinder. It made her feel vaguely triumphant, like an explorer or mountaineer, high up on top of the world. It was only when she jumped down, five minutes from home, and began walking on the dusty road, that she became aware of something behind her. At first she thought it was the heat, playing tricks with her mind, creating something out of nothing. But then the shimmering became a discernible movement, then a more distinctive bodily presence, following her, not far behind, getting closer. And suddenly there were two people, thrusting their faces into *her* face, and laughing. They belonged to Vivienne Carter and Lorraine Best. Ester had never seen them on her way home before, nor had she ever exchanged a word with them in class. But suddenly they were here, palpable, insistent, on this dusty road. She was perplexed, and slightly afraid.

It was Vivienne Carter who spoke first, drawing herself back so that she seemed even bigger, putting her hands on her hips:

'Why, if it isn't Ester the Pester! Fancy meeting you here. Are ya on ya way home?'

Ester understood that this was not a real question. Where else would she be going at this time of day? She wanted to say this, but somehow the sharp sound of Vivienne Carter's voice and her standing there, hands on hips, the heat, the sudden dryness in Ester's throat, made it all too difficult to speak. Instead, she smiled, what she hoped was a polite smile, and stood fixed to the spot. This time it was Lorraine Best who spoke, with the same malicious edge in her voice as she drew closer:

'Ester the Pester, why don'tchu speak when you're spoken to? Didn'chu your mum tell ya to be polite?'

Again Ester felt the foolish grin on her face and now a churning in her stomach, that inexplicable and sickening sense of having done something wrong. And there was something else as well, more frightening and foreboding—the intuitive and utterly certain knowledge that they meant to do her harm. Not just a tug of her plait or a jeering laugh, but something altogether more difficult and alarming. She felt the clamminess in her hands and a racing racing racing in her chest and it was all she could do to start walking steadily steadily, hoping that by staying calm she could make them go away, leave her alone. But instead they ran ahead and jumped in front of her, making scaring booing noises and waving her to a halt.

Again it was Vivienne Carter who took the lead, and this time her voice had a steelier ring, cold and slow and thumpingly insidious:

'You're such a know-it-all, aren't you, little Ester? Teacher's pet, always stickin' your hand up in class. *What's the capital of Istanbul, Ester? "Please, Miss, I know, I know. I know how to do sums and say poems and I can even write 'em. There's nuthin' I don't know."*'

And now Lorraine Best chimed in, with a light sing-song that gathered weight and gravity with each sentence:

'Think you're too good for us, don'tcha, with your stupid plait hangin' down your back and your stupid la-di-da dresses and your fat face. Well, if you're so smart, why'ja eat those stinky samwiches with that stupid fatty meat inside 'em and that yukky smelly cheese that stinks up the class all afternoon? And why'ja have such a stupid name? Ester Sloshki? What sort'va dumb name is that? Sounds like snot, all snotty and rotten. You think you're smart, but you're not, you're just a smelly smelly, Ester the Pester, smelly belly.' Lorraine Best smiled slowly and turned to her friend.

Ester knew these words were silly. She wasn't smelly, she didn't have a fat face, she wasn't stupid. She knew who was stupid, and she wanted to shout back at them, *I like what I eat and I like my name and I like to know things and I wish you would leave me alone.* But when she looked at them and saw their big hard bodies and the menace in their eyes, she felt as if her tongue had been cut out, like the girl in the story about the nightingale, and she knew she must get away. She started to run, stumbling in her fear, terrified of some nameless hurt, hoping beyond hope to reach the gate where she knew her Mutti would be waiting. But she was too slow and they were too fast and Lorraine Best caught her by the arm and pinned her in a bear hug and squeezed her hard, so hard that Ester felt her insides red and burning. Vivienne Carter stood in front of her, her hands swinging at her side, and it was then that Ester knew. She saw close up the meanness of her face, the coldness in her eyes and in her heart; she saw the fist thrust towards her and she felt the blow, hard and sickening and somehow very dark.

And then everything went still. Ester felt the blood running out of her nose and saw it dripping onto the ground, bright red drops, one after another, separate and distinct. Vivienne Carter and Lorraine Best looked vaguely shocked, but it was difficult to say why. Three frozen figures, a dusty, mute and bloody tableau, a mirage in the heat.

Ester moved first. Slowly, and then unstoppably, her whole body shook—shoulders, torso, arms and legs, all the way to her insides. Her tears wouldn't stop, streams and streams of tears running down her face, mixing in with the dirt on the road.

And her words came out at last, they had to, it was the one word, over and over again—*Mutti, Mutti, Mutti, Mutti*—sobbed out childishly, a helpless incantation of pain, bewilderment and loss.

Aroused by the word, Vivienne Carter and Lorraine Best once more found their voices—nasal, mocking and unrepentant:

'Mutti!' they echoed as one, 'Mutti, Mutti, Mutti!'

And again, 'Mutti, Mutti, Mutti!' soaring in the heat and the dust.

Halfway through the nightmare

How can we measure that which is immeasurable? How can the unfathomable dark be divided into two neat halves?

Driving on the freeway to work, Hannah couldn't stop thinking about the sign. She'd been keeping strictly to the speed limit, periodically checking the traffic in her rear-vision mirror, wondering about her in-tray—all those crisp pages stacked up neatly, the folders in an orderly pile—and aware of the ribbon of river out of the corner of her eye. Then, from out of nowhere, there it was, hanging down from a pedestrian overpass—a tattered white banner with large black lettering, bold and furious, proclaiming: HALFWAY THROUGH THE NIGHTMARE. You couldn't miss it: it was declarative, insistent, its words dripping like so much black blood, framed by defiantly jagged edges, fluttering in the wind. Motorists honked their horns, but whether in amusement or sympathy was impossible to tell. Of course Hannah hadn't been able to stop, even if she'd wanted to. She had no choice but to keep on doing 110 kilometres an hour, keeping just enough distance between the car in front and the car behind. A few kilometres more or less and you could be dead.

Hannah was still thinking about the sign, those words, as she stepped into the lift and pressed the button for the thirty-ninth floor. The elevator glided up smoothly, as always. There was no need to panic; the movement was barely perceptible. Of course, she told herself, the sign might be a joke—the work of some amateur philosopher, perhaps—the kind of prank that existentialist uni students might play, if the mood took them. But then again, it might be serious. Did it signify a breakdown? An empathetic message to the similarly afflicted? Hannah was aware of the sickly green glow of the elevator button, the mirror-bright space around her, and realised that it was the halfwayness of the nightmare that had so unsettled her. Was this a sign of resilience, she wondered, a stoical belief that an end was in sight? Or mere resignation to a life of replicated misery? She found herself thinking about the person behind those words. What might he look like? How long had he been up there? It would have been freezing on the overpass, early in the morning. The man would be hunched over in the cold, buffeted by the wind, his hands in the pockets of a thick dark coat. Hannah heard the familiar 'ding' of the elevator—the muted announcement of arrival she knew so well, and which she vaguely dreaded. She felt the discreet bump of the landing, heard the elegant swish of the doors opening onto fields of soft blue carpet. Hannah's heels sank down as she made her way to her office. She saw her reflection, abrupt and sharp, in the glass door and thought, with a start: what might it feel like to be a shattered self? Something, she knew, was nudging at her, asking all these uneasy, these treacherous questions.

The rest of the morning was mostly routine paperwork. Mondays were the worst days: lawyers' phones in meltdown after a weekend of domestics, split-ups, custody disputes. There must be something about weekends, Hannah thought, which brought out the worst in people, or which simply brought them out, made them confront the unspoken conflicts, express the anger, the needs, the hurt, beneath years of carefully tended marital pretence. Her colleagues referred to Monday as the Day of the Flayed, the Frayed and the Mislaid, and couldn't understand why she didn't like the joke. She thought they were cruel; they thought she was humourless. Not just any kind of humourless, of course, but a particular and derisory kind—middle-aged spinsterly humourless, no less. Hannah was under no illusions about what they thought of her. The ones who'd worked here a long time, as she had, used to think she was *enigmatic*. She'd been told this by a junior partner years ago, at one of those shamefully boorish office parties when everyone is stupidly drunk, flirtatious and indiscreet. She'd also been told, at these parties, that she was beautiful; and that a beautiful young woman who was quiet and reserved was, naturally, bound to be enigmatic. Now that she was fifty, she was simply certified *remote, aloof,* even *stuck up*. Words overheard in corridors; read on a misdirected email. Hannah was glad it was Friday. Fridays were usually saner—reason was being restored and the law was taking charge, taking over. She was looking forward at the end of the day to the solitude of her garden, to the serenity of the sequestered space she had carefully, lovingly, cultivated over the years. Perhaps a drink or a movie with Shona on the weekend; a visit from her favourite niece. That would be nice, and enough.

It was lunchtime already, Hannah realised, watching various colleagues heading off to the bistros and cafés that jostled together in this part of the city. People left in recognisable pairs or groups. Mitch and Wallace, new boys in their new, dark suits—still slightly glossy, both the suits and the boys, shiny like drycleaners' plastic. And new shoes, of course, similarly glossy, impeccably crafted. All that youthful confidence. It was the walk, wasn't it? The long-legged, almost arrogant stride, but not too fast, everything measured. Acting the part. Mitch and Wallace had certainly got it right. Edward, the boss, as well: a slow, deliberate walk, as though deep in thought, with a hint of menace in the set of the shoulders. The walk of uncontested professional power. And the female partners too: an upright posture; brisk, no-nonsense steps, with a subtle sway of the hips—a remarkable accomplishment, really, and one that Hannah knew she'd never been able to perfect. Not that she'd ever tried.

She rose slowly from her chair, feeling suddenly rather heavy, drained. As if the mere thought of lunch was a burden. She'd long ago stopped eating in those bistros and cafés with her colleagues, elbow to elbow with laughing people who often seemed to laugh for no reason at all. She hated the wall-to-wall noise, the ugly clatter of china; the overpriced food and the chilled mineral water in long, pretentious glasses. And going out for lunch, out of the building, meant coming back, going up again. Thirty-nine storeys. These days she usually ate in the tearoom, an even more welcome space since the disappearance of the tea-lady, with her spuriously matey airs. Today, this particular Friday, Hannah wasn't alone. The new man was there again, looking through the window. She'd exchanged a few words with him yesterday—John, his name was: a name as unremarkable as the man himself appeared to be. Forty-five or fifty, perhaps, with grey hair and grey eyes, and what Hannah had already decided was an undiscriminating geniality, an all-too-ready-made smile. He was standing now with his hands in his pockets, rocking slightly back and forth on his heels. Hannah walked to the table and sat down, trying not to make a noise. It was easy to be quiet in this room, she told herself, biting into her sandwich; easy to hear nothing but the slither of the lettuce and tomato slipping down her throat.

The man, John, turned from the window and smiled broadly at her, as if he'd known all the time that she was there.

'Is it possible to tire of this view?' he asked rhetorically. Hannah had always disliked rhetorical questions; she regarded them as a waste of words, an invitation to nothing. She smiled feebly in return and looked down at her sandwich; strands of lettuce were spilling out of the bread and she tucked them back in.

'Just look', he continued, 'at the sweep of it all. Those microscopic shops and parks and then all the lifting spires. And the river snaking through the city.' Quite a speech, Hannah thought dismissively. And he was waving his hand rather extravagantly; was he trying to impress her? Was this a move? Then he laughed, an embarrassed laugh, making less of it all. 'I'm sorry, you must be bored with all this gloriousness.' The light streaming through the window seemed to cut through his face, almost cut it in half. She felt him concentrating his attention on her. 'How long *have* you been working here?'

A question that required an answer, Hannah knew. She sensed that he might be nervous—was she right, *was* this an overture, a beginning?—and she replied curtly:

'Twenty years. I don't look at the view because I'm scared of heights.'

She looked down at her sandwich and up at the man. Dissected by the sunlight, his face seemed both remote and oddly compelling. She was conscious of his presence across the room, the long lean slope of his body framed by the window; this, and something about his rather boyish brightness made her, suddenly, want to say more. 'I used to be afraid and then I learnt not to be. One has to work here, after all.' This seemed somehow insufficient, now that she had begun. 'I try not to think about where I am, how far up...' Hannah stopped, but it was already too late. She flushed as she saw him approaching the settee, now rubbing his hands lightly together, with an air, perhaps, of anticipation. His face appeared in full before her, his unremarkable, friendly face, smiling above her. She knew she'd gone too far.

He was sitting now, his legs crossed comfortably. He was relaxed, undoubtedly more sure of himself, more sure of her. Hannah began to feel a slight flutter, that low-grade swirling in her stomach whenever the elevator started its silent, inevitable ascent. How can he be so sure of himself, she thought resentfully. Or sure of me? Such certainty was presumptuous, even preposterous. And then, out of nowhere—holding her soggy sandwich, seeing the man's long lean legs and the light through the window—she suddenly felt an alarming urge to cry. This was not like her at all. Sensible, her family had always called her. Someone who never acted on impulse, who kept herself to herself, as her Auntie Madge would say. Who carefully observed the speed limit, knowing one false move could be your last. But now—it was extraordinary—caution seemed to have abandoned her, and she wanted nothing more than to drop her head in her hands and sob. She wanted to be folded in this man's arms, feel his steady hands stroking her head, hear him saying, 'There there, it's alright.' Instead, she looked down at her own hands fidgeting in her lap and said, stupidly,

'I saw a sign this morning.'

There was a silence. Hannah felt mortified. What on earth would he think, think of her? She was so afraid he might laugh. So she rushed on, more earnestly than she'd intended, 'Oh, I didn't have a religious conversion, if that's what you're thinking.' At this point, he *did* laugh, but whether in relief or slight contempt she couldn't tell. Perhaps she'd offended his religious sensibilities; perhaps he thought her a bit of a baby, this middle-aged woman in a well-cut, dark grey suit and neat dark hair, whose face was hot, whose hands were clammy with disclosure. She could see her half-eaten sandwich lying on her plate.

And then everything seemed to change again, in an instant. John reached across the table and took her hand. This unknown man; it was as simple as that.

'Something's distressing you, isn't it?' he asked gently. His smile had disappeared.

It was the word *distressing*. He hadn't said *bothering* or *upsetting*; he knew, instinctively, with troubling precision, exactly what to say. And so when he went further, when he said, 'Tell me about the sign', something, everything, returned to her, one more time. That distant wave, barely visible, far out to sea, which was always there, which would sometimes swell and rise and rush towards her, sweep her up and tumble her around, turn her over and over. John removed his hand from hers, still leaning forward. His face, she saw, was open to her, opened up.

And so her story could begin.

'His name was Jonno,' she told him. 'We were eighteen; it was our first year at university. I'd met him in the coffee shop. It was difficult to talk, I remember—there was always so much clatter and loud laughter—but I heard enough the first time to know that he was different. Intense. He told me I was ravishing, that he wanted to eat me up. Just like that. He leaned across the table and started nibbling my face. And then he got down on his knees and proposed. He was so long and gangling, all legs and a lean, whippet body. He told me that he refused to go to war, that he was going to be a conscientious objector if his number came up. He'd had a huge row with his father, who'd thrown him out of the house. I remember him looking at me closely, his eyes narrowed, and I wondered whether this was a hint, whether I was supposed to offer him a home, some temporary refuge, in the future. I simply nodded, in sympathy. I hardly knew him, after all.'

Hannah was looking across the room as she spoke, staring at nothing, and she could feel the man's eyes on her as she continued.

'Jonno took to sitting with me in the coffee shop. His talk was sometimes rapid-fire, sometimes dreamy, far away. He was a drama student and a wonderful mimic, a great impersonator of politicians and movie stars. It wasn't just his skill with voices; it was the way he marched or strode or meandered, imitating perfectly the gait of the famous, the notorious. Once, I remember, he told me that the walk was everything. *Get the walk right*, he said, *and you've got the whole man*. And then he stood up in the crowded coffee shop and starting playing Mussolini, with his staccato strut. He—Jonno—was very funny. I liked him because he was so uninhibited, so free. I was a shy and nervous girl; afraid of life, although I didn't know it at the time. One doesn't know such things. But Jonno made me laugh, and I liked to hear him talk. He sometimes spoke quietly—so quietly that it was difficult to hear him—in a faintly bookish manner. He would look at me intently, for long periods, silently. Once he said, 'We're wonderful together, aren't we?' I was flattered and excited. We often went for walks along the river. We held hands and didn't always feel the need to talk.'

Hannah had to stop, fearful of what was to come, fearful for Jonno and for herself.

'Then he started talking strangely. His conversations became monologues, more and more rambling and difficult to follow. On one particular day, in the coffee shop, he wouldn't stop doing the Mussolini walk. He kept goose-stepping—flamboyantly, frenetically—and then he started yelling, louder and louder, in a mock-Italian accent. His voice rang so clearly, above all the chatter. It wasn't funny this time. His eyes were wide, so wide; it looked as if he would never close them again. I remember people trying not to watch him, and then looking at me because I was with him. Wondering what to make of us. I can see them now, all the students in the coffee shop. I think that's when I decided to stop seeing him as well.

'Then I heard rumours: he'd started roaming the streets at night, shouting out obscenities and intimidating people. He was found one day prowling the corridors of the Arts building, knocking on doors and screaming, threatening violence. People locked their doors, shut themselves in, and someone called the police. I saw him one more time, near the library, walking towards me, but I quickly turned the other way. At least I think I did. I'm not sure if I'm making that up.'

Hannah could hear her voice quavering with the swell of shame.

'A few weeks later a friend told me that Jonno had been found lying dead on the freeway. The news report said that motorists had seen his body falling from the overpass, his arms outstretched and flapping like a bird. Cars slammed on their brakes but it was too late. And I remember that I said to my friend, to Shona, that I was glad I didn't get too involved with him. *Anyone who thought he could fly, fly like a bird*, I said, *was obviously mad.*'

Hannah looked across at the window and forced herself to feel the drop, down down down, thirty-nine storeys. The room seemed to darken momentarily and she tried to feel what Jonno felt, perhaps, on that night when he flew, flew like a bird in search of some terrible freedom. And then she dropped her head in her hands and sobbed. She could feel the man fold her in his arms, feel his steady hands stroking her head, hear him saying, 'It's alright, Hannah, it's alright.'

Some time later, perhaps a long time, Hannah withdrew from this man, this stranger, and tried to recompose herself. She straightened her jacket, brushed back her hair, rummaged in her bag for a tissue. This is what people did, what people do, she thought, in scenes of distress. She felt foolish, yes, and undignified, but undeniably and mercifully returned. As though she had been dumped on the shore by a tumbling wave and left gasping for air; exhausted, but safe. Alive.

'Have you never spoken of this before?' Hannah heard the man asking. Again his words were exactly right. Here there was no presumption; no intrusion. His voice was soft and low.

'Only once,' she replied. And then she blushed. 'Although you'd be forgiven for thinking this was the first time.' He was looking at her closely. 'I spoke of this to my friend Shona, years later, just after our graduation. It somehow seemed right. We had become close friends—she is still my oldest, my dearest friend—and I think I felt the need to apologise, for my ignorance, my callousness; for what I said when Jonno died. For what I didn't say when Jonno was alive. I wanted to let her know that I could be a better person than the one who cast away so cruelly this poor, this lost young man...You know...things haunt you, mark you, fill you with such self-reproach. Such things never leave you, do they?'

'And what did your friend say?'

Hannah paused reflectively.

'Nothing. Well, not quite. I remember that she held me in her arms and said my name. It felt like a blessing.'

'As indeed it was.'

Hannah liked his manner of speaking. Gentle, and rather formal. Attentive. She wanted to tell him that Shona was the kindest person she had ever known. Instead, and instinctively, she reached across the table and placed her hand on his.

'Thank you for your kindness,' was all she said.

She found herself thinking about her garden, walled off from the noise of the freeway traffic, and how she would sit there tomorrow with Shona and talk, or not talk, in the sun. And how she might tell her, without being asked, that she had met a man, a quite remarkable man, named John.

Meteor Man

Look at the stars! Look, look up at the skies!
O look at all the fire-folk sitting in the air!
The bright boroughs, the circle-citadels there!
Gerard Manley Hopkins, 'The Starlit Night'

They say that everyone has, or should have, a special moment in their life. Like the words to that song, 'Camelot'. Yes, I know it's about kings and knights and a world far away, and I know my kids prefer the hammy Spamelot version, but in a funny kind of way it's about all of us really, all hoping for one of those brief shining moments. And me, Frank Marvell, I'm no different. I've seen life shine at certain times, or at least I think I have. And who's to say that I won't see it again?

My marriage, for example—it will be twenty years next April. You don't get to be with someone for that long, after all, without there being some highlights. Like the first time I saw Angie. We'd been introduced by a mutual friend at the Teachers' College where she was studying, and straightaway I liked her crooked smile and the golden flecks in her eyes. She was wearing a big hat, sort of perky and floppy at the same time, and covered with orange flowers, and she was standing under a tree with the sunlight—dappling, I think it's called—dappling her face, so I could see the sprinkle of freckles on her cheeks and nose. Like magic dust, it was. The next few months were a bit of a blur really, of restaurants and movies and, one special night—Angie's twenty-first—dancing under the stars. A number of her student teacher friends had already become engaged that year—the Dip. Ed. Diamonds, they called themselves—and so the next step was obviously to buy Angie a ring and pop the question. She accepted, thank goodness, and it was settled. I do remember feeling slightly uneasy during the church service—a sudden moment of panic when the priest asked *Is there anyone here…?* but I suppose I thought that was normal. We honeymooned in the Barossa Valley and it all went pretty well. To be honest, I'd only slept with one woman before—a fairly rushed, fumbling business, really—and Angie was a virgin, so it was all a bit awkward on the first night. But things improved as the honeymoon went along and over the next week I never tired of seeing the shape of my wife's beautiful breasts under her nightgown. There was just enough moonlight to show me their fullness, their curve, waiting to be touched.

We've had our differences of course, like most couples, but we've travelled along pretty well together. We know each other, we know what to expect, and the steady glow that comes from security, from stability—that's not to be dismissed, is it? It's true that our sex life has never reached great heights, but then I suppose it's like that for most married couples. It's nice enough, and there's never been any question, for either of us, of an affair. Several of our friends have been unfaithful and their marriages have either fallen apart or been repaired, but Angie and I are content to keep on going as we are. I still enjoy her smile and the golden star-flecks in her eyes, and when she's asleep next to me I like to listen to her peaceful breathing. Sometimes I find myself reaching over to touch her face, gently, so as not to wake her. To be honest, Angie's never been particularly interested in sex, and for some years I found this quite difficult. It's not that she's cold, exactly. But she isn't—passionate, I suppose. Then again, maybe passion's only for the film stars, like that dark Welsh beauty I quite fancy—Catherine somebody, the one with the double-barrel name and the long black hair. Anyway, it's become easier, as most things do. I've learnt to—contain myself, really; learnt to accept that's the way things are. Angie and I rarely argue, and when we do, it's over trivial things, or sometimes money. We both like to garden, and we're proud of what we've created in the front and back yards. So much colour—roses, marigolds, hollyhocks, wisteria on the fence. A riot of reds, oranges, purples, pinks, through every window of our house.

And then, of course, there's our kids, Terry and Tessa—the other lights in my life. Terry is the first-born, born only ten months after the wedding, in fact. Both his mother and I found the early months rather difficult. He was a colicky baby, screaming for weeks on end and refusing to sleep for long stretches, day and night. It was something of a shock, I can tell you, and it upset me to see Angie crying as she tried to soothe the fretful child. I tried patting and rubbing the little mite, but felt foolish and clumsy, at such a loss. Angie once confessed to me that she felt as though she'd *fallen into a big black hole* that she would never climb out of, and I remember feeling proud of the way she'd soldiered on.

Terry grew into a nice little chap, fond of his sport and just a bit cheeky. We did the usual things—kicking the footy, flying kites, riding a bike. The first time he managed to get a kite into the air, and keep it there, he'd run faster and faster, shouting from a distance: *Look, Dad! Look how high! I'm going to make it disappear into the sky!* I loved the excitement in his voice and the idea of his kite sailing up and up, the string getting longer and longer, magically, floating away until it was only a faint orange dot, the tiniest speck. It was one of those moments you have sometimes, both ordinary and remarkable—your son, a kite and an endless blue sky.

Tessa was born two years after Terry and was a much easier baby. In fact, she was an absolute joy right from the start. I know that parents aren't supposed to have favourites, but I have to admit that Tessa's always been very special to me. Maybe her birth had something to do with it. I was there, and I can say without a shadow of a doubt that it was one of those astonishing moments, little short of a miracle. I'm embarrassed to say that I wasn't much help with the birth itself—for a bloke, I'm pretty squeamish when it comes to blood. But when I held this tiny creature in my arms, I was—well, completely stunned. I think I stopped breathing for at least a minute. And then I cried. This little being was so curved in, so perfect, with her fuzz of black hair and Angie's crooked mouth, and I swore she looked straight at me as if she already knew who I was. I remember a big wave passing through my body—it's the only way I can describe it. I had no idea where this feeling came from, or the tears; no one had prepared me for any of this.

So what else do I remember about her? A lot to do with water, now that I think about it. Water seemed to be Tessa's natural element. I took her to swimming lessons when she was still crawling and I loved holding her up in the pool, my arms around her fat little tummy, as she kicked, squeaked and splashed. She was never afraid, just slap-happy and laughing. *Poppie, Poppie,* she would squeal to me in her tiny, high little voice—like crystal, it was—and I felt so proud, buoying her up, her support, the difference between life and death. Oddly enough, she was much quieter in the bathtub, almost meditative, you could say. She would lie there forever, so still, while I gently scooped bubbles at her, soaped her up, carefully lowered her into the water to wash the shampoo from her hair. I used to smile at the chubbiness of her, those little rolls of fat on her arms and legs, and her marvellous little face surrounded by a comical halo of froth.

And then, somehow, things started to change course, as they seem to do. I can remember the day, in fact, it was when Tessa was three years old, the day we had Geoff and Gina round for a barbecue. I'd been talking about the way I loved giving Tessa her bath and I remember Geoff giving me a funny look and saying he'd *stopped doing the bathtime thing* with his daughter. *It feels a bit funny now, you know, washing around her private parts, I let the wife do it now.* I'd never thought about this before and somehow it didn't seem right to think this way. But next bathtime, I felt clumsy and sort of guilty, and found myself washing my daughter much more quickly than usual, wrapping her up tightly in her bright orange towel. And that was the end of it, really: Angie took over from then on, while I got tea ready. I was a bit sorry about all of that, but I suppose I knew there was nothing to be done, that there was no going back.

Still, over the years there've been other shared pleasures with my girl. I've ferried her to dancing lessons and watched her move more gracefully with each year. Once she danced the part of an angel, spreading her fairy wings, looking so tiny and serious. She was a speedy swimmer too; she powered through the water, as if she was moving through air. It still takes my breath away every time I think of it. Later she switched to netball. She had an impressive leap on her, I remember—the highest in the team. And then there were the high-school concerts, which I always watched feeling puffed up with pride. Angie and I would nudge each other when Tessa tap-danced solo or high-kicked in the chorus line of *No No Nanette* (of course she was the best dancer and the one with the biggest smile).

At some point—I don't remember exactly when—Tessa stopped calling me Poppie and I became, instead, just Dad. She sort of went her own way, as kids do, as they have to. She had lots of friends who seemed to spend most of their time painting each other's fingernails and looking at those celebrity magazines with pictures of scrawny girls with the names of faraway places, silly names like Paris and Sahara. Tessa talked a lot with her mum, as is natural, I suppose, and she made it pretty clear that teenage girls don't really want their dad hanging around too much. I remember how they'd sometimes stop talking, she and Angie, when I came across them having some secret pow-wow, laughing together, or Tessa crying sometimes. I still went to every concert and every weekend netball game, and we still shared some hugs and pecks on the cheek, but you know when something's being lost, is lost, although if you'd asked me then, or even now, I wouldn't be able to tell you exactly what it was.

So now, here I am, forty-six years old. Frank Marvell, finding myself with more and more time to think about my kids, Angie, our lives together, those twenty years that seem a long, long stretch of time and yet are over in a flash. Where's it all gone? Take this evening, for instance. I'm standing in the kitchen watching the kids horseplaying, with that physical and verbal banter they enjoy. Terry, all of six feet two but unable to grow the beard he desperately wants, putting his sister in a gentle headlock as she calls him Mr Bumfluff. Him teasing Tessa about her ambition to be a model, the way she spends hours in front of the mirror cultivating what Angie tells me is *the look*—a kind of blankness, eyes staring straight ahead, right through you, in fact, and a slightly sullen set of the mouth. I think she looks like an alien and a few days ago I made the mistake of telling her, not exactly in those words, and she stomped into her room and wouldn't even come out for dinner. *Doesn't matter,* Terry had shrugged, *she's trying not to eat anyway. One of the girls at school said she needed to lose a couple of kilos.* I hadn't meant to be unkind. It was just that her face had upset me, and I'd blurted it out before I knew what I was saying. She looks so—dead, really, her face painted white, with those expressionless eyes. I don't think *the look* is beautiful at all. In fact, it's sort of creepy; my daughter's like a creeping thing, not herself at all.

And there are changes in Terry too. He's so much bigger and louder. Like all his uni mates, he seems to fill any room he walks into. Door frames shrink and it's like there isn't enough space inside for his big, muscular body. And it's all that confidence I find so astonishing. These boys—young men—they all seem so easy in their skin. They swagger; they sort of preen. I feel somehow smaller in their presence, almost invisible, as they eat and drink and laugh and occasionally speak to me in tones I can't quite make out:

'Hi, Mr Marvell, how's it going? How was work today?'

Now I know this sounds innocent enough, even friendly, but the politeness seems somehow—not forced exactly, but slightly mocking, as though these hulking boys are making fun of the good manners their parents have taught them, as though good manners are unbecoming to their sense of self. Or maybe, as Angie would say, I'm seeing things the wrong way again. She used to be a schoolteacher, so maybe she understands teenagers better than me, keeps things in perspective. Oh they're good kids, for sure, and I'm pleased they haven't fallen in with a bad crowd, like some of them do. They probably think I'm a nice enough bloke, if they think of me at all, just Terry's dad, no more, no less. And Terry, what does *he* think of me? It's hard to tell, now that I ask myself the question. Terry has a kind of mask these days, like Tessa, something you can't quite get through. It's like they aren't quite there. Or I'm not.

It was like that at dinner last night, an air of something changing, something wrong, as though the world had tilted ever so slightly. I've always insisted on the family eating together at night, and much of the time we do. What with our busy days—work, study, domestic chores—it's a good chance to catch up with one another. Angie had made one of her delicious meals, and the rhubarb pie—my favourite—was a triumph, the pastry a little soggy, just how she knows I like it.

'That was a great pie, Angie, one of your best.' I'd sat back in my chair, dabbing at my mouth to remove a speck of cream, but the moment I spoke, I was aware of the smiles exchanged between the kids. What had I said? Was it wrong to compliment my wife on her cooking?

'Hey, Dad, you've got a bit of cream on your chin.' Terry had pointed to the offending item.

'Thanks, mate. Shows how I want to savour every mouthful.'

Again the smiles. Was I being—*what* was I being?

There'd been a moment's silence, and then Tessa, her shiny bracelets tinkling on the kitchen table, had leaned over to her mother:

'Oh Mum, I forgot to tell you that I've decided to go vegetarian. Not strict; I'll eat some eggs and dairy, and lots of fish for the Omega 3, but definitely no meat. Our human biol teacher says that animal fats are really bad for your cholesterol levels and we have such high rates of heart disease in this country. And anyway, I think we eat far too much meat in this family. I'll help you cook some new fish dishes, Mum, I promise.' She'd smiled her crooked smile.

Angie had looked interested and smiled in return. 'I'll be in on that, Tessa. It'll be good for *me* too. I need to shift those kilos from the holiday down south.'

'What about ethical reasons, Tessa?' I'd asked her, wanting to get past the jangling bracelets and that bit of smugness in her voice.

'Dad, weren't you listening?' she'd said, eyebrows raised. 'I said I'd eat fish, so it can't be for *ethical reasons*. Fish are living creatures too, you know. And eggs and dairy come from animals as well.' She'd paused, looking past me, into the air. 'And there's another reason of course. My teacher says that a no-meat diet helps stabilise your weight. Animal fats are really bad for putting on weight, and the last thing I personally want is to get into that yoyo dieting, lose it, gain it, lose it again. It's very bad for you.' And she'd folded her napkin decisively.

But something in me hadn't finished with this.

'But why do you want to lose weight in the first place, Tessa?' My daughter wasn't fat—or was she? I'd never thought so, but how could I tell?

And Tessa had laughed. 'Oh Dad, you're such a dork,' was all she'd said, as she left the table, making her move.

I'd tried to laugh with her, sound amused, thinking that amusement might be the right response.

'What's a dork?' I'd asked.

Then Terry had joined in the laughter. 'Dad, it's exactly because you *are* one that you asked that question.'

Tessa grabbed her brother's arm. 'Come on, Terry, I need you to give me a lift to the library, remember? I'll be ready in five minutes.'

And they were off, playfully punching each other as they left to go to their other lives.

Angie stood up from the table, clearing the dishes.

'Those two. They like to tease. But it's nice to know they look after each other, that they're actually good mates.' She'd nodded to me as she swept past. 'We're lucky, you know, hon. So many kids these days seem to be on drugs, or this binge-drinking that you read about in the paper all the time. But ours are basically good kids. They've never given us any major headaches.'

She was right of course. There was nothing to say to that. And then, as I too stood up from the table, carrying dishes, I suddenly felt—you know, that odd, from-out-of-nowhere feeling when your heart suddenly drops inside you, and then you find yourself sighing, for no real reason. I wanted to put my arms around Angie, my wife, have her arms around me, but she was already leaving the room, hardly turning to look at me as she said something about *popping off to Nan's*. I'd remained standing in the middle of the kitchen, vaguely aware of the sounds of the house settling, creaking, and the wind outside. I'd heard Angie's car backing out of the driveway and realised that I hadn't even heard her say goodbye. The noise of the wind was louder and I felt tired and even a little annoyed. The kitchen curtains were still open and I remember seeing the black sky and a full moon. I'd roused myself for a moment, thinking I should get started on something—there was something I was meant to be doing—but I found myself doing nothing, simply standing there, looking up at the sky.

So now, it's a week later, and I'm driving home from work after a meeting. I still feel tired and not really myself, if you know what I mean. It's like being weighed down, anchored to the earth; as if the rhythm of my life—a kind of steady hum—is changing. Something's being hollowed out, as if things no longer matter as much as they had, or should. Over the week I'd tried to tell myself that I was being stupid, worrying about nothing, but none of this could stop my unease and a troubling sense of being on the verge of tears. I grip the steering wheel more tightly, concentrating on the road ahead. And then suddenly—it's literally in the blink of an eye—I see this amazing streak of light, high up, so high, a fiery streak hurtling across the sky at a furious speed. So startling, so bright, so dazzling, a glorious whoosh of beauty, orange against black, moving faster and faster, lighting up the darkness. I almost cry out as I watch and then gasp as I see it plummet down and down, as rapidly as it appeared, still glowing, so spectacular, so golden, and utterly miraculous. And then just as suddenly it vanishes. There's simply no trace of it in the black night sky.

I have to stop the car to get my breath back. I can't quite believe what I've seen. For just one moment it feels like the end of the world has arrived, terrifying and beautiful at the same time. My hands are still on the steering wheel; I can feel their clamminess as I put them in my lap. Of course, I tell myself, it was a meteor. What else could it be? But I never knew they could be like this, so brilliant, so marvellous, a long streak of blinding fire like a message from another world. I realise I'm shaking, ever so slightly, and I look up at the sky again to confirm that this blaze of light had been there, was real, was there for everyone to see.

I wait for a while to collect my thoughts, then turn on the ignition. As I take the road again, I find myself driving faster, feeling anxious to get home, to tell those I love what

I've witnessed. I'm excited, unsettled, as if somehow I've been saved from something, as if I've been close to death and lived to tell the story of my miraculous escape. I pull into the driveway of our house, reassured by the glow of light in the window. Scooping up my briefcase, closing the car door, locking it, I steady my breathing and walk calmly to the front door and into the house. There they are, as I know they will be, my wife and children watching television, the lights on the screen flickering in the darkness. I can see Terry hugging his stomach with laughter, Angie sewing and Tessa curled up next to her on the sofa, eyes fixed on the TV. No one turns around. I know I can't hold back any longer.

'Hey everyone, guess what?' I find myself speaking more loudly than usual. 'I've just seen the most amazing thing...You wouldn't believe it!' I put down my briefcase and wait for them to turn around, to look at me, to ask a question.

Angie and Terry swivel around and give me a smile, while Tessa remains staring ahead at the glimmering screen. I know I have to speak, to stand between them and the TV and point to the dark sky outside.

'I've just seen the most marvellous meteor. It was incredibly long, really fast and fiery orange, so fierce and dazzling, it looked like it could blow up the whole world!'

My arms drop to my sides and I stand suspended. There's a silence, and then my son seems to speak for them all:

'Get away, Dad, anyone would think it *was* the end of the world! A meteor is only heated space matter, you know, a bolide, they just burn up and disappear.' He turns back to the TV screen. Tessa's still curled up on the sofa, playing with her toes. Angie half-moves to get up and asks if I would like a cup of tea, as if that's what I really want.

The next morning I'm sitting alone at the kitchen table, wondering what I should, or could, be doing. Suddenly Tessa appears in the doorway, Tessa with her crooked smile. She seems to have come from nowhere, in a sun-coloured dress and her face lit up with the brightness of the day. But before I can speak she's gone, quick as a flash; I barely have time to register her cheery wave and the glint of her shiny bracelets. She simply disappears from the room, her voice trailing off into the distance:

'Hey, Meteor Man, I've got modelling class after school today. Will you tell Mum I won't be home for dinner?'

Looking out to sea

I am floating on my back in the ocean. The water is calm and warm. If I open my eyes I can see the clouds, wispy, grey-white, streaky, with holes in them. I can feel the heat of the sun on the parts of my body not covered by water: my face, my stomach, my toes. I know there is an island in the distance, but of course I can't see it; you have to look hard to see it, even from the shore. The waves today are tiny, hardly there at all, and I feel myself gently drifting, weightless, but not a dead weight. I am alive, because I can feel the movement of the water, the sun on my face. When I close my eyes I can blank out the clouds, the sun, the sky and simply float, float, float, as if forever. I sometimes lie like this, on my back, for hours, but I always leave the water when it begins to get dark. The twilight is one of the worst times for sharks, they say; but it's not the sharks I'm afraid of.

Two days ago I had lunch with a colleague and someone I didn't know, who didn't know me. Why should she know me, as she'd never met me before. We went to the café where I've been coming for two years. I had the smoked salmon and a glass of chilled white wine. The waiter is a handsome young man, with laughing brown eyes and a heart-shaped, rather sad face, if you can imagine laughing and sad belonging to the same person. I know he is nineteen years old, because I asked him once, not long after I began coming here, and he was seventeen then, so he is nineteen now. On this particular day I keep losing the drift of conversation, I keep looking at the baby at the table next to us. She's sitting in a high chair between her parents, waving her spoon in delighted circles and banging it on her mother's nose. She is one of those sunny babies, for whom it is a joy to be alive, and she has a spiky fuzz of light brown hair lit up by the sun. My colleague's friend leans over, tapping me lightly on the arm. She asks if I am *getting clucky, wanting a grandchild?* I see my colleague give her a look that tells her she should change the subject.

We were married for many years and for some of that time we were happy. Then we started to become unhappy. I can't really remember when it started, the unhappiness, because of course there is no particular moment when love stops. It seems to be this way for many people. They begin by adoring each other, wanting to be together all the time, wanting to touch each other all the time. Then they become irritated or bored or angry or frustrated, or whatever it is people feel when they fall out of love. At first we tried to rescue the marriage, and did the things people like us usually do: counselling, telling each other our feelings, going out on romantic evenings. But it wasn't working. It probably wouldn't have worked anyway, even if it had never happened. So now we live apart, although we're still officially married, probably because it seems like too much trouble to get a divorce.

My sister, whom I love, was very worried about me. She used to check up on me every day, she would phone me to ask if I was alright. Most of the time I didn't say much but I was glad to hear her voice. She would talk about grief in an abstract and general way. *Grief is very complex and personal,* she said, *we never know what form it will take or how long it will last.* Once I became upset on the phone because that morning at work I had overheard a woman say *it was selfish for people to go on mourning for ages.* She may not have been referring to me, and she didn't say how long *ages* was, but I knew she could never have felt grief. When I told my sister, she said, *Don't listen to other people, listen to yourself. You'll know when it's time.* I couldn't say that I felt it might never be time, that it might never stop.

I remember the bruises, the bleeding, the grazes on shins and knees. The falls from bicycles and skateboards. The toe that was squashed under a slamming door; the howl, the red rawness of it. The child who fell out of a tree and was mercifully caught by his father, hovering below. His body lying on the hospital bed as they wheeled him away for his tonsillectomy. Eight years old and tiny in a shower-cap and gown, his hand waving bravely, calling out cheerily, *Don't worry, Mum.*

There are so many photographs. In one of them he is standing on the driveway, dressed in his green and white uniform, holding his schoolbag in one hand and waving with the other. He is smiling, but because he's leaving home he also looks sad, so he looks happy and sad at the same time. There are photos at fancy-dress parties and teenage parties, and there are many of him as an elfin-faced baby. I stare at these particular images for such a long time that it seems I can almost touch his baby body, cradle it and rock it like I used to. Those were the years when he would cling to me, feeding and tugging and demanding, those years when a mother's body is not her own. Now my body is my own and I find that it's not what I want.

I remember the first night he went out driving, in his father's car. He waved out of the window because he knew I was watching. Although he didn't want me to watch, he still waved, because he knew it would please me. He was like that. I was so frightened that I lay awake until two in the morning, until I heard his car pull up in the driveway. I couldn't stop imagining: the deadly swerve at the corner, the head-on collision, the body lying on the highway. These, I'm told, are perfectly normal fears. Of course it was better over time, although I continued to sleep fitfully and was always relieved to hear him coming home.

I remember his first girlfriend, his only girlfriend, the girl he couldn't stop touching, he was so besotted with her and with being in love. He helped her buy clothes and choose a new hairstyle. When she stayed overnight, he always took her breakfast in bed—scrambled eggs and bacon or muesli, carried carefully down the stairs on a lacquered tray, with a flower picked from our garden. I would hear his laughter, her laughter, as they settled into bed to share the food. Once she appeared at our door, sobbing, and I saw him fold her in his arms, not speaking, just holding. They would always kiss each other goodbye. I remember thinking that his was the first generation that could die from having sex, but when I said this to my husband, he told me that it wasn't normal to think this way.

I have a friend, a painter, and last year he asked me if I would like him to paint a picture for me, of anything I liked. I wanted him to paint a picture of grief, but I didn't ask him, because although I knew the colour of grief, I didn't know how he, or anyone, could paint a picture of what isn't there.

Yesterday my husband paid me a visit at work. He asked me out to lunch because, he said, he wanted to see how I was getting on. I knew this was very kind of him, he didn't put any pressure on me for anything else, didn't make any demands, he just wanted to know how I was getting on. We went to the place where I always go and I could see my husband looking at the waiter, puzzling over his face, thinking he must know him from somewhere. It was a pleasant lunch and the food was, as always, very good. My husband waved to the waiter for the bill; he insisted on paying.

It is still not easy to read, although I have always loved reading, especially novels. I can usually follow the plot and understand the characters, but I still have to be careful about which books I choose. I think they're going to be about some particular thing and they turn out to be about something else, something I hadn't expected, something unbearable. When this happens I have to stop reading. I used to believe that reading could be about recovery, but now I am not so sure.

Earlier this morning his girlfriend phoned me to see how I was getting on. We keep in touch regularly. I am very fond of her. She is a lovely young woman, very kind. She has an uninhibited laugh and the most beautiful yellow hair, which glows when it catches the sun. She has another boyfriend now but we have become friends and this will never change, regardless. I'm lucky to have these people who call to see how I'm getting on. My sister, my husband, my colleague who takes me out to lunch, my son's girlfriend, are all very kind to me.

He wasn't sure what he wanted to do with his life. He'd just finished school. He told me that he was too exhausted to think much at all. *All that study, Mum*, he said. *My brain is frazzled.* He would listen to music I didn't know—garage bands and soul—and plunder my record collection for long-forgotten sixties songs. Once I was passing his room and he pulled me in, grabbed me around the waist and danced with me, laughing, telling me to *loosen up, Mum, let yourself go.*

Sometimes I think about what must have happened that night. I try not to, but of course you do, how can it be helped? He and some friends had gone to the beach because they wanted to see the water at night, they said, wanted to feel its mood. They were like that, he and his friends. They told me later that my son said he'd always wanted to swim to the island, that one day he would do it, and they'd laughed and said he'd have to get into training first. After a while they went off to buy some food, leaving him alone on the pier, looking out to sea. When they came back an hour later, they saw his shirt but couldn't see him anywhere and so they thought he must have gone home. But of course he never came home and no one ever found his body, probably because it had been washed out to sea. I try not to think about that night, but I often do. Sometimes it feels like I think about it all the time. I think about his body. I picture it, lying in the water, face down, and then slowly sinking. I know people think this is morbid, to see such pictures, but I can't help myself.

I often come to the beach because I have to think it will help, and sometimes it does, floating on my back, closing my eyes and letting the gentle swell of the water hold me up, bob me up and down, side to side, in a slow, soothing motion. When it begins to get dark I leave the water, wrap myself in a towel and sit on the shore, looking out to sea. I would like to be able to stay in the water, at night and floating, letting myself drift, looking up at the stars. It will happen sometime, soon or later, I don't know when, but I know it will happen.

All the girls are doing it

Later, she would see this as a defining moment. When brutal words were spoken. When she saw her lover truly, for the first time. When all her good fortune was reversed. None of this was as she'd imagined.

They were choosing names again, or rather, Ruby was trying to decide on a name for their baby. All girls' names—Ruby was sure it was a girl, just a feeling she had. It was following the same pattern: her suggestion, his joke.

'What about Isabel?'

'Is a bell necessary on a bicycle?' Joe smiled.

'Susan? I've always liked that name. And it's not all that common now.'

'Soosin' down your leg,' he said, pleased with himself. It was what the boys at school used to call his sister.

'Well, Louise then,' Ruby continued, undeterred. 'Another lovely, old-fashioned name. Make something of that, will you?'

'Loo wees in her pants,' Joe pronounced triumphantly.

Ruby smiled, despite her mild irritation at her lover's schoolboy humour. These silly puns reminded her of some of the guys at her old school, all greasy sexual nudge-and-wink. Not that Joe was sleazy, or in the slightest bit unattractive. On the contrary. He was what her girlfriends called *drop-dead gorgeous*, with his *dreamy brown eyes* and rather knowing smile. Even the scar on the side of his face was sexy. Ruby could still remember the night they'd met. It was one of those movie-moments she'd seen many times—eyes across a crowded room kind of stuff—with Joe asking his mates to introduce him to that good-looking blonde, and Ruby swept away by what her mum later described as his *matinee idol good looks*. And there was, she'd thought at the beginning, just a touch of Romeo and Juliet about it, given his parents' objection to the match. Joe was in his final year of an engineering degree; he was a young man going places, she knew, superintelligent and ambitious. Ruby had been told this often enough by his family and friends in the year they'd been going out, become a couple. Joe was aiming for a job in Sydney, in one of those office towers, all glittering glass and silver, with what the ads called *panoramic views*. She and Joe had laughed together when they first saw those promotions on TV, with their transformation of the world into so many sheets of gloss, such blinding shine.

But now the idea of Sydney was less appealing, even a little troubling. And they hadn't told anyone yet. Ruby wanted to be sure the pregnancy was stable; and besides, it wasn't going to be much fun breaking the news to Joe's parents. He'd hugged her, of course, and then smoothed his hands over her belly, unable to speak, while *she* was longing to shout out the news, sing it in fact, to her own mum and dad, her sisters. But with Clive and Christina she wasn't so sure. Less sure with each passing day, another day when Joe didn't raise the subject. His parents had made it pretty clear—never in so many words of course, but it wasn't hard to tell—that a girl who'd left school at sixteen, who cut hair for a living, wasn't quite the right thing for their son.

But here they were, a year later and still together. Most of Joe's friends, she knew, thought it wouldn't last. He had a reputation as a bit of *a pants man*, she'd heard his mates call him, when they'd had a bit too much to drink. Even when—especially when—they knew she was listening. But they'd proved them wrong, hadn't they? It *was* partly the sex, of course it was; they could never get enough of each other. Ruby would finish at the salon and pull open the door to his flat, calling out his name, and he'd be there instantly. There'd been other partners, but she'd never had sex like this before, that made you want it again and again. Even now, there was sometimes something furious about their lovemaking. They ripped at clothes, scratched, sucked hard, bit hard. She wanted it never to end.

But it was more than sex, despite what Joe's mates seemed to think. She'd seen the way they looked at her, well, not at *her* really. They'd already made up their minds. Joe had told her that one day, she wasn't sure why really, but whatever the reason, she'd felt hurt. His friends didn't know her, didn't know the slightest thing about her. And no one knew what she and Joe had together, they didn't have a clue. How could they? You couldn't know someone in a bar, or by the clothes they wore, or their hairstyle. Knowing was lying in bed for hours, not talking, just touching. It was having him inside her, so deep she couldn't tell where she began and ended. Knowing was loving the imperfections of his body, like the large red birthmark on his back that she would kiss and kiss and kiss again. And knowing was saying things you wouldn't talk about to anyone else. Like telling Joe she wanted to have her own salon one day and design the interior, not with the usual pictures of wide-eyed models with sculptured hairstyles, but with art works, like the Picasso she saw in a book, the painting called 'Girl with Yellow Hair'. Ruby had showed it to one of her clients one day, but Mrs Foss had shrieked that the girl's hair looked like a cockatoo's. Ruby had wanted to tell her that this wasn't the point, she wanted her to see that the entire painting consisted of only one line, one wonderful brush stroke. How could anyone do that, she'd wanted to ask. She couldn't say that to her client, but she could say it to Joe.

And he told her stories as well, especially about his love of bridges. Ruby guessed that he never spoke like this to any of his friends, that he kept this particular passion, like the sex, just for her. He told her about one of the most famous disasters in civil engineering history, the collapse in 1940 of the Tacoma Narrows Bridge. 'It was bloody spectacular,' he said, waving his hands about, surprised she'd never heard of it. 'It was the third largest suspension bridge in the world at that time, and the largest in America. It had a main span of 850 metres—pretty damn long for those days. And Ruby, it was one of the most beautiful bridges you could ever hope to see—so elegant, so streamlined, like a—a testament to lightness and graceful movement.'

Ruby loved her lover's transformation of the bridge—all that solid steel and concrete—into an airy dance. And she was keen to know what happened, even though he'd more or less told her the ending. She wanted to know how and why.

'Well, it collapsed because of wind-induced vibrations. It couldn't withstand the forces of nature. The strength of the vibrations caused the collapse of the central concrete supports, and then within minutes, a one-hundred-and-eight metre section broke out of the suspension span. And that was it, really. Once the central span had gone, there was nothing to balance the weight of the side spans and—down it went, down went 'Galloping Gertie'. Amazingly, it was all captured on film, you know, by the owner of a local camera shop. I'd have given anything to have seen it, recorded it. Professors all around the world still show the video to students as a kind of cautionary tale.'

'Do you mean it was a warning to engineers not to get too confident, too sure of their own success?'

'Well, yes, certainly. And to highlight the fact that engineers have—quite literally—the lives of other people in their hands.'

'And in this Tacoma Bridge collapse—did anyone die?' Ruby had felt the weight of responsibility in her lover's words.

'I don't remember actually. I don't think so.' He was tugging gently at her hair, focused on the coda to his story. 'In any case, a lot of good came out of it. Civil engineers and architects had to consider new theories of vibration, aerodynamics, wave phenomena and harmonics, which led to much better designs, better construction. A second and much safer, longer bridge was built there ten years later, and now they're working on an even better one. It'll be finished in a couple of years.' He smiled as he twirled her hair. 'So, out of ruin and disaster, new knowledge, better ideas. Even when there's been loss of life, like the collapse of the Melbourne Westgate Bridge, much closer to home. I remember that because my parents used to talk about it—Dad had worked with one of the architects, actually. Thirty-five, I think it was—construction workers—were killed. But the important thing was that engineers learnt from their mistakes. New and better structural designs, new methods of construction; we're getting better all the time.'

Ruby had drawn back a little, trying not to think about those thirty-five men who were crushed or drowned. She listened instead to Joe's exuberance, his sense of vision, the sweep of his sentences affirming his belief in progress. This was a man, she knew, in love with his work.

So, on this morning, choosing names, she could afford to indulge her lover's childish sense of humour. How could she possibly be annoyed? She felt magnanimous, embracing. She loved this man ferociously for making her feel so ripe and content, for giving her this life inside her. For she was more than just herself now: she understood this completely. She was transformed, made anew. Her body had a secret knowledge; no, it was knowledge itself. The slight curve of her belly; the deepness inside. No one could see this yet, but she knew. Joe knew. She would touch her breasts and feel them magnificently full. She felt greedy for sex, she wanted it all the time, hungrier than ever with their baby growing inside her. She'd already begun to imagine what she'd look like in four or five months' time. Her belly would be large, tight as a drum. Oh how she longed to look like that, how she couldn't wait. She would walk proudly, her head in the air. She would wear tight-fitting shirts, and low-cut dresses to show off her beautiful breasts, spilling over. They would be full of milk, to suckle her baby, full and lovely for her lover to touch, to cradle in his hands, to kiss.

So she gave a name for their baby one last shot. She wanted something special, something that Joe couldn't turn into a joke.

'I know—let's call her Pearl. Then you'll have two precious jewels, mother and daughter.' And before he could respond, Ruby moved towards him, holding his head and drawing it down onto her, asking him to lick her nipples, suck them gently.

She moved against her lover and arched her back, wanting more, guiding his hand under her dress. She whispered to him, *Make me come, over and over and over.* She could see him watching her, waiting for her, as his hand stroked her, but he seemed to be just watching. She drifted away from him, concentrated on her pleasure. He was already moving away as she stretched out her arms, feeling sated.

That night they cooked dinner and talked about what they'd do on the weekend, after Joe had finished his last assignment for the term. As Ruby made the salad (feeling absurdly elated by the colours as she tossed the vegies into the bowl—luscious reds and bright greens, vibrant oranges), she couldn't help but bring the conversation back to the baby. Just as she couldn't help seeing babies everywhere she looked. There seemed to be an armada of pregnant women that she'd never noticed before. Big-bellied, confident women, gliding through the streets. Magnificently curved, upright in their pride. Why did no one stop and stare at them? And she hadn't known there were so many shops selling baby clothes, tiny jumpsuits and frilly pink knickers, so tiny it was hard to believe that any creature could be so small. She saw chubby babies, drooling babies, babies kicking their legs in pushers or peeping out from a mother's shoulder; doll-like baby legs dangling from slings. It was like being in love: everything referred.

'Mum and Dad will be so happy,' she told him. 'They've just about given up getting grandchildren from my sisters, and they idolise you, you know.' She brushed his lips softly with her fingers. 'They already know how smart you are, what a great cook, and a potential gold mine, and of course that you love me madly. And now they'll add to that list what I already know—that you're the most fertile, spunky, life-giving man on earth.' Ruby felt light-headed and flirtatious, spilling out girlish words to this man she adored. She reached over and slid her hand down her lover's trousers, but he gently removed it and set about cooking the meal.

'Not now, Ruby,' was all he said.

She sensed a sharpness in his voice, a new note, like the look in his eyes when he'd satisfied her earlier in the day. She dropped the flirting routine and began to sound serious.

'What's wrong, Joe? Did I say something wrong?'

'No, of course not,' he replied, not looking at her. 'I'm just a little on edge. You know my parents aren't going to be too impressed.'

Ruby picked up a crust of bread and popped it in his mouth.

'I know that, of course I do. I know they have plans for you, to go interstate and work, and I know they'll probably think a baby will get in the way. But even if we *do* end up in Sydney, I promise you a baby won't change anything. I'll see to that. There's no reason why I can't take most of the load, all of the load. It just won't be a problem. And as soon as they see the baby, Joe, as soon as they see their grandchild, you know their hearts will melt. How could it be any other way?'

She took his hand and smoothed it over her belly, guiding him, wanting him to feel the warmth, this newness, inside her. 'This is our baby, and there'll never be another baby like this one, ever again. Your parents will come round.'

She waited for him, willed him, to speak.

'Sydney isn't like this place, you know,' he said, as if he were about to tell her another one of his stories. And then he looked at her oddly, sharply. 'You know, Ruby, I've never really heard you talk like this before. You sound so—well, so gushing and maternal. I didn't think you'd be one of those girls who gets like this over a baby.'

Ruby was taken aback. Like what? How was she supposed to feel? Was it wrong to feel—what had he said?—*gushing and maternal*? Wrong to feel that everything was perfect, that her body was rich, so rich that right now nothing else—silver towers and salons and girls with yellow hair—mattered much at all? Now he'd said that something was wrong and his face, she saw, was glowering and unsure.

That night, in bed, Joe turned his back on his lover. There was a silence between them and Ruby shivered, despite the heat of his body. She wanted to hold him, to touch him; she knew that if she touched him, it would be alright, everything would be alright. She slid her body next to his, fitting snugly, warmly, into his back. She reached over and slowly stroked his neck, his chest, gently squeezed his nipples. As she reached his stomach, she could feel his back arching. She moved her hand down and cradled his balls, the way he liked it. She waited for him to turn to her, to want her. Instead, he moved further away from her, silently, making a cold space between them. Then he sat up, abruptly, and turned to her after all:

'For Christ's sake, Ruby, don't you ever get enough? This is what got us into this mess in the first place.'

This, then, was the precise moment. When particular words can never be unsaid. Something sounded inside her head—she heard it, she felt something move, like a dull thud; and something closed down inside her. It was like a shutting down. She thought, this is what it feels like when your heart breaks.

Joe must have seen the look on her face, the blankness, for he drew her to him, wrapped his arms around her and stroked her hair, almost wildly.

'I'm sorry, Ruby, I'm so sorry. I shouldn't have said that, you know I didn't mean it.' She could hear the panic in his voice. But it was already too late. She pushed his arms away and glared at him, tumbling out ugly, wounding words before she could stop herself, not wanting to stop herself:

'So, it's my fault I'm pregnant, is that what you think? I'm like a bitch on heat, a fucking rabbit, screwing all the time. I'm a slut, am I? I can't get enough, don't you ever get enough, Ruby?—that's what you said.' Her face was blotchy and red, unpretty, all streaked with tears.

Again Joe tried to take her in his arms, but she pulled away.

'I didn't mean it,' he said again. 'I didn't know what I was saying. I'm just tired, and worried, you know, of course I don't think that...'

She didn't wait for him to finish his sentence, and now her voice was steely, cold. 'But you said it, Joe. It's what you *thought*, what you think. Do you think I don't care about you? What about your pleasure, our pleasure? Why do you think I want sex, Joe, what exactly do you think I get out of it?' She'd never spoken to him like this before, so sure of herself, so sure of everything.

Joe ran his hand through his hair.

'Of course I know you think about me, Ruby. I know you care about me. But sometimes I feel like you're on a—well, a sort of power trip, it's like you want sex when you want something. And I don't just mean an orgasm, I mean when you want your own way, so you turn me on, you get me excited, so I'll give you anything...'

'Bullshit!' Ruby screamed at him and then drew herself up in the bed.

'So this is what it's all about, is it? Me on a crummy power trip, having sex to make a baby you don't want, to get you to keep a baby you don't want. All this is a *mess*, is it?'—she said the word slowly, scornfully, her hands smoothed over her stomach, enclosing, excluding—'My baby is a mess, is she? Like a piece of garbage, a pool of vomit? Is that what you really think?'

Joe buried his head in his hands. Neither of them could say anything, dared to say anymore. But then he looked up at her, his face burning, and forced himself to speak.

'I don't really want this baby. You know I love you, and you know I want us to have babies, we'll have lots of them, three or four, more if you want. But not now.'

He waited for her response, but she remained silent, her hands still resting on her stomach, her breath suspended. She heard his voice again..

'Ruby, I'm only twenty-three. And—I have such good prospects, so many plans.'

Then he sobbed, once, with the enormity of what he'd said. She looked past him, icy and unforgiving.

'Say the word, Joe. You want me to have an abortion.'

He looked up at her, his face flushed with the guilt of relief. He summoned the courage to take her hand and his words came more easily.

'Please don't think I'm being selfish, I just think it's the right thing for either of us. We're too young, Ruby, I haven't even finished uni yet. And what about your salon, the one you said you always wanted to own? It's just not the right time, not now.'

She watched his hand stroking hers. She looked closely at the hairs on his arm. He was talking somewhere in the distance, she knew, talking to her, saying things to her in waves of muffled sound. She heard his words go up and down, up and down, in shifting tones, the edginess in his voice giving way to calmer, steadier notes, and she knew that he was taking her silence for consent. She saw his hand reach out to touch her face.

'I'm sure it'll be alright,' she finally heard him saying. 'I know our doctor would be happy to do it, and it won't be too hard, I'm sure it won't. Lots of girls your age have them, for all sorts of reasons.'

He paused and gave an uneasy laugh, a discordant prelude to his closing words:

'I even heard someone saying the other day, it was some guy in parliament, that girls have them to look good in a bikini.'

They stayed together, although she didn't really know why. Perhaps she was simply tired, unable to move away, move anywhere. They talked less. The sex was subdued, even, at times, sombre. Joe remained attentive, doting on her every minute he could spare from his studies. He completed his degree, the outstanding graduate in his field, and began making plans for Sydney. She continued to cut hair, shampoo and style; she had no one's life in her hands. Joe's optimism, all his vision and faith in the future, no longer held her up. Whatever was between them now, she knew, could collapse at any moment.

And then in the month when her baby was supposed to have been born—she did this deliberately, knowing now that she wanted to be cruel—she told him she was leaving, and unlike their families, he understood why. He tried, one last shot, to change her mind, to win her back. He bought her a ring, an elegant diamond, on the strength of his prospects. She opened the blue velvet box, then snapped it shut, shut like her heart.

For the rest of her life, she continued to think of him, think of that time—their youth, their happiness, their unhappiness. How could it be otherwise? But she recovered, lived her life, gave birth to two daughters and a son. She never owned a salon, but she learnt about Picasso and saw the girl with yellow hair in another city, all glittering glass and silver, with panoramic views from her hotel room. But there was loss, irreparable loss: she always remembered the boy who loved bridges and the thirty-five men who were crushed or drowned.

Cobbler, cobbler

We sat together, my mother and I, cross-legged on the floor, looking at family photographs. So many of them, stuffed into cardboard boxes, waiting to be sorted, perhaps discarded. This was meant to be a speedy task—part of a hasty spring-clean before moving house; but the webs of nostalgia had caught us in images of gurgling babyhood, my spindly adolescence, my mother's towering beehive and doleful panda eyes. Among this jumbled narrative of growing up, growing older, there were only three photographs of my grandmother, this woman who'd always shunned the camera's unlying eye. One pictured her as a bewildered immigrant standing on the wharf, protecting her eyes from the glare of an unknown sun. There was a holiday snap in King's Park, with a gum tree in the background; my grandmother sitting decorously on a picnic chair, wearing her best dress and string of pearls. And one image from those final years, when the illness that secretly ravaged her, that no one saw until it was too late, was already etched on her face.

My mother held the picnic photo closer to the light and said wistfully,

'There's no doubt she was an ugly woman.'

I saw my grandmother, fixed by the image. Her ugliness was indeed remarkable, the stuff of fairy-tale: all pointed and protruding teeth, a large hooked nose and wiry hair matted into jagged clumps. Befanged and butchered; the Evil Stepmother. But she was also the woman who had rocked and cradled me, sung me to sleep, slipped me forbidden sweets; who had shielded me from schoolyard taunts and broken hearts, from the heat of the sun and the furious winter's rages; who was for me the shape of love.

My mother turned over the photograph, as if to find the real woman on the other side, hidden from the camera's cruelly impersonal eye. Her voice took on, suddenly, the mysterious tone of a significant offering, some secret explanation of a life lived, or hardly lived at all.

'He married her because she was ugly,' she said. 'And then he kept her so.'

Over the years I had been told almost nothing about this grandfather, my grandmother's husband; and I had never asked. A child learns not to, catching glimpses of strained faces and overhearing whispered words. There were no photographs. He was merely a name—Gustav. He had died long ago in a land far away, across oceans of time. He had nothing to do with my grandmother at all. Here, now, on this August evening—the sky outside a velvet black, inside the hush of memory—my mother's words had sketched him into some kind of ominous life.

'Tell me about him,' I asked her, leaning my head on her shoulder. I was again a child, wanting above all a story and the soft maternal presence enfolding its narration. I had always loved my mother's night-time tales, read from books or created in her head. She gave me a world of fantasy creatures—malevolent goblins in cobwebbed dungeons; haughty queens and armoured knights on heavy-footed horses; gruff-voiced trolls under creaking bridges. A world of mysterious objects: poisoned apples, glass slippers, golden caskets. Night after night, all this magic and melodrama, suspense and romance, was made especially for me. And always shaped by a happy ending, for a child settling down to sleep and dreams. But this story, I knew, locked away in the attic of my mother's past, would be different. A true story; much more disturbing, and inescapably real.

'I don't quite know where to start,' my mother said, her mouth a line of faint distaste. 'But I should warn you,' she added, without a trace of irony, 'it's not a pretty tale.'

'Your grandfather', she began, 'was a proud man. He rose from humble origins—he was a cobbler by trade—and through his business acumen and chivalric charm, soon made his way in the world. When he met my mother—your real grandmother— he was only a young man, but already wealthy, with a gold fob watch glinting against his prosperous belly. Her beauty enthralled him. He was completely captivated. You've seen the painting of her—those dark, caressing eyes, the high cheek- bones and forehead, a porcelain skin like a perfect mask. A full, sensual mouth.'

Of course I'd seen this, seen her, many times. The painting hung in my mother's study, on the wall opposite her desk. Every time she glanced up from her work, my mother must have seen this smouldering beauty, gazing upon her as if she were alive. She must have felt her haunting presence as she tried to think and write. As a young child, I would sometimes drift into the room and study the painting, running my fingers around the ornate frame. Once, I remember, I'd left a note on the desk that read, *I love the princess in the paining*. My mother had laughed gently at my childish mistake, but I had seen the sadness in her eyes.

'My father courted her relentlessly for many months,' she continued, 'competing with dozens of suitors from neighbouring cities, before finally winning his prize. He had made a great deal of money. Enough, at least, to buy my mother, to adorn her bare white arms with diamond bracelets, her graceful neck with delicate pearls. She was, quite simply, breathtaking, as if especially made for the sparkle and luminosity of jewels, the rustle of embroidered gowns. And your grandfather, make no mistake, was a handsome man, with an upright posture, piercing eyes and a full, ripe mouth. The kind of mouth which women—some women—mistake for voluptuous generosity. He wore his wealth weightily, rigidly, in his bearing. I never once saw him bend.

'Not long before I was born, barely a year after my parents were married, my father commissioned a portrait of my mother. As confirmation of ownership, no doubt; as visible proof of his fertility. Of course he never used such words to me, but I can see the stamp of masculine pride in the composition and colour of the painting: the swell of my mother's belly beneath her midnight purple gown; the faint half-flush along her throat; the full breasts. Specially commissioned breasts.'

I heard the mockery, the edge of contempt, in my mother's voice; and in the pause that followed, I saw once more my grandmother, the Ugly Stepmother, in a long-forgotten scene. Stark and framed, as if set apart. Inexplicable, and vaguely shameful. Sitting on her bed, naked from the waist up, her large pendulous breasts hanging sadly down. I had heard noises coming from her room and tiptoed to investigate, bright-eyed with childish curiosity. I peeped through the crack in the door. There she was: old; obscene; pitiful. Stroking her breasts and weeping softly, moaning in her native tongue,

'Why did he have to die and leave me? So long, so long, my man is gone.'

'Are you listening, Katchen?' I heard my mother ask. 'I was telling you about your grandfather's shoes.'

I had missed a thread in the narrative, but as my mother resumed, I fell once again, easily, into the spell of her story.

'He owned a highly successful shoe shop,' she said, 'which pandered to the whims of the pampered bourgeoisie. His style became legendary throughout the city. Elegance was his trademark: dainty pointed toes and heels, slender straps and intricate buckles; shoes of pearly pink, moss-pale greens, powder blues. So tiny that they barely covered the palm of a man's hand. In time my father was summoned to the Court and asked to make bejewelled slippers for the Princess. His crowning achievement. He didn't *make* the shoes, of course, any of them. He designed them. They were made—hand-made—by a team of women who worked long hours, their backs bent, their eyes straining, their fingers aching, in a dark and cobwebbed room. Now I know it as sweatshop labour; but for the child I was then, many years ago, the place had all the enchantment of an elfin grotto, cavernous and musty, hidden underground. I visited a few times with my father, who would circle the women inspecting their work, peering sternly over their shoulders, knowing what to look for. He was always straight-backed, silent and imperious.

'I don't know if he and my mother were happy before I was born, but I know they were unhappy when I was a child. I would like to think there were moments of pleasure, of laughter and brightness, some youthful delight in the newness of it all. But what I recall is my father's wrath: his purple face and stomping feet, his huffing and puffing like a large Rumpelstiltskin—a thwarted, apoplectic child. He told his wife to lower her gaze when walking in the street, to cover her arms with a shawl, to stop smiling at other men: *Your smiles are snares!* he shouted at her. *You must only smile at me.* He called her names I didn't understand, and she would run away. Her feet were not tiny, I remember, and they were very fast.

'And then, one day, he hit her. I was under the kitchen table, licking the cake dough from a large glass bowl; a serious child of four or five, swirling the chocolate mix with studious concentration. This was my mother's special task for me: *Lick it all up, Gretta,* she would say, *and then we won't need to wash the bowl.* This was one of our little jokes, one of the few things I remember about her. That morning, under the table, I saw nothing; but I heard the blows—one, two, three—swift and strong; pounding flesh. I heard my father bellow, *Devil! Devil! Devil!* each time he punched her. I heard my mother's terrified screams—*Gustav, stop, please stop! The baby!* And then a moaning, a body folding up on the floor, and small whimpers, like a wounded kitten. I kept cleaning the bowl, slowly, noiselessly, licking the dough from my fingers. The mix was so thick and so sticky. I heard my father's footsteps, hard and unforgiving, on the floorboards, heard the door slam, heard the strange silence that he left behind. There is much after this that I can't, or perhaps won't, remember. But to this day the smell of chocolate cake makes me sick, makes me want to vomit, as I did then.'

I could see my mother's eyes wet with memory tears. She was again the fearful, stricken child, hearing the ugly world from beneath a kitchen table. I kissed her cheek, softly. I kept my mouth on her face, tasting the sweetness of her skin. She patted my hand and drew up her shoulders, a grown woman, my beloved, my beautiful mother, ready to resume her ghastly tale.

'I never saw my mother again,' she said. 'It was only years later that I learnt the truth—that she had hemorrhaged massively, lost so much blood, and lost the baby that my father had wanted so badly to destroy.' My mother's face was reddening with the slow burn of accumulated anger. 'One night, years later, when he was very drunk, he had a screaming fit—I heard him from my room, a hideous ogre demanding vengeance, wanting only to kill. He shouted out ugly names about my mother, venomous words. He shouted out the names of men in the town. When I woke up in the morning, I saw a bottle of vodka tipped over on the table, a pool of white liquid on the floor. We never spoke of it. Perhaps my father didn't know I had been there, had heard everything, both then and long ago—his lunatic jealous ravings and my mother's piteous cries; the anguishing silence of a room filled with the stench of vomit and blood. I left home a few months later, as soon as I could.'

My mother's voice was subdued. Her anger had disappeared, like many things, in that faraway land. But I was angry for her, and for my grandmother, this unknown woman in the painting. I pictured her there in the past, as she watched her face every day in the mirror, smoothing her spun-gold hair; adjusting her shawl, her smile. I could see the mirror crack, split into silvery shards, with the terrible curse of beauty.

'Why wasn't he caught, this monstrous man?' I asked my mother, helplessly. 'Surely people must have suspected? Wasn't there an autopsy, an investigation?'

My mother smiled grimly. 'Ah, you see,' she replied, 'Gustav was the town's pre-eminent cobbler, whose beautiful shoes—those elegant, tiny, intricate shoes, worn by princesses—put money in the city coffers. Brought tourists flocking to his shop. Such gifts, it seems, are priceless.' She turned to me and sighed. 'You see, Katchen, I warned you—this is not a pretty story.'

'But you haven't finished yet,' I protested.

'You used to say this every bedtime,' my mother smiled. 'Always wanting to prolong the hour. *Keep going!* you would insist, *don't stop now.*'

'I wanted to keep you with me just a little longer,' I confessed.

'I understand,' she said quietly, drawing me closer. 'And you're right—this is not the end of the story. Your grandmother. Where does *she* belong in this sorry tale?' I saw my mother's deep brown eyes, the lustrous eyes of her mother, take in again the photograph in her hand. 'I know very little about this part of my father's life, about our beloved Oma as his wife. I didn't see him for ten years. I wanted never to see him again; he was hateful in my eyes. I found a job in another country, where nobody knew him, or me. I made friends and a new life. Sometimes, in the night, in that space just before sleep—when you remember all that has made you, all the years drifting up towards you like a dream—it was possible to believe that he had never lived at all.

'But then I heard that he was very ill, that he was dying. A message was sent to me from a cousin, who had somehow managed to track me down. To return me to my father's home. *Gretta, please come*, she wrote. *It is your father's dying wish to see you.* The letter was full of news about his illness and about the woman who had attended him for the last two years—his new, his devoted wife. When I sent no reply, when I didn't make the journey home, another letter came. This one was simply one dark line, bewildered and accusing. *Have you no heart?* my cousin wrote. And so, with anxious expectation, I went back. My father was indeed very ill. Weak and wasted; in the care of this new wife, this woman of startling ugliness who fed and cleaned him, stroked his brow and smiled through her sorrow. When I saw my father's gentleness towards her—his tender voice, his gestures of gratitude—I was almost moved to tears. I watched them over the next few days—her endless kindness, the way he patted her hand, kissed her softly on the mouth—and I felt something shift in my heart.

'And then one day he shouted at her. As feeble as he was, he raised his voice enough to denounce her *vagrant ways*, her all-too-friendly smile. He demanded that she cut her hair. This woman whose already greying tresses were hanging down, limp and lifeless, around her skinny shoulders. *Chop it all off!* he ordered, trying desperately to rise in his bed. *Go to the barber's and have it all chopped off.* And then he sank down into his creamy white pillow, gasping faintly, *I don't want those men to look at you.* The next day she stood at his bedside, shorn and penitent, her hands crossed meekly in front of her apron. What had I expected from this man, my father—this sickly, tyrannical weakling, folded up like a limp rag doll? A deathbed conversion? A seeing of the light? I laughed inwardly, sardonically, at my hopefulness; and I cried openly, for this piteous ugly woman whom I later came to love. I didn't stay long enough to hear my father's dying words.'

'Where did he find her?' I asked.

'Where you would least—or perhaps most—expect,' she said, putting down the photograph at last. 'In his cobbler's workshop, in the underground. She was one of the women whose backs were bent, whose eyes were strained. When my father chose her, singled her out from his aching squad, he must have known already that he was eaten up inside. And what must *she* have thought, to receive this blessing? To be rescued from such wretchedness, to be married to such a handsome, wealthy, powerful man? She told me once, years later, that she used to sing when she was working, before her magic transformation, that she would tap her little hammer on the cobbler's last and sing, *At last, at last, my prince has come.* The other workers would laugh at her dreadful joke. They were, no doubt, speechless when he did—finally—arrive.'

'So was she happy? At least for some of the time?' I wanted this to be my final question.

'Ah Katchen, I don't know,' my mother replied. 'We rarely spoke of him after his death. There must have been many things which neither of us wanted to disclose. But I saw how she doted on him when he was alive. And I saw her eyes smile whenever he touched her. Perhaps he was the only man to have touched her, ever, with some kind of tenderness or desire. Who can say, for another, what happiness is?'

I recalled my grandmother, the one I had seen through the treacherous crack in the door. Her old, sagging breasts; her plaintive cry, *So long, so long, my man is gone.* I took the photograph from my mother's hand and kissed my grandmother's face; kissed her goodness, her sadness, her abjection, and the glimpse of a happy ending on her pointy-toothed smile. The clock struck midnight. The photographs—memory's precious, most evidential texts—were still scattered on the floor, still waiting to be sorted. There was nothing to be done, now, but to kiss my mother too, and climb the stairs to bed.

A comedy of manners

A child should always say what's true,
And speak when he is spoken to,
And behave mannerly at table:
At least as far as he is able.

Robert Louis Stevenson,
A Child's Garden of Verses. V. Whole Duty of Children.

They were, as usual, reading different sections of the paper. Philip was scanning the stock market details, while Grace was immersed in the headline story. He was entirely silent; her tongue was making faint clucking sounds of disapproval.

'You know, Philip, I really don't know what's happening these days. It says here that road rage among the young—not just young men, but girls too—is on the rise. Last month alone there were fifteen incidents, three of which resulted in serious physical injuries to the victims. And one of them was an elderly woman: isn't that disgraceful?'

Grace peered over her spectacles, seeking the moral comfort of spousal confirmation. Philip's slight nod was all that she required.

'It's the violence that's so shocking,' Grace declared. Her voice began to huff with indignation. 'According to the Commissioner, the police have had to break up four parties already this week, and then they were pelted with rocks and cans for their trouble. Just look, Philip, look at this picture—all the broken bottles, and these imbeciles brandishing fence pickets. It's so ugly, so frightening. I ask you, what's going on in the world?'

When Philip continued to keep his head down, Grace was forced to answer her own question.

'Oh, I know these are extreme cases, Philip. But nevertheless it's hard not to notice a general decline in civility, in manners, among the young. Pushing and shoving in queues. Swearing in public. I heard a young man in the supermarket yesterday talking to his mate about the *f-ing girl* he'd been out with the night before; apparently he'd had an enjoyable dinner at a restaurant, but it was *f-ing this* and *f-ing that*, right in front of me. The language of love, indeed. And we could certainly use some manners on public transport. You should see the children's faces when the driver makes them get up! There's one in particular, a lad who always mutters at me under his breath if he's forced to stand. He's from that local school, you know, the one that's been having a lot of trouble with truancy. Not that bad manners are the prerogative of the public system, of course. Do you know, yesterday on my morning walk, I was just about bowled over by some private school girls, walking three abreast on the footpath, refusing to move over. Smartly dressed in their blazers, boaters and ties, but there they were, swearing like troopers, elbowing me out of the way. So immaculately turned out, and so very rude.'

Grace paused briefly as she considered expanding on her theme by way of illustrative contrast.

'Is it only older people who understand the importance of good manners? Take the drapers, for example—you know, the ones who've just closed down after nearly fifty years. Lovely lovely people, always so helpful and polite; two generations of service they've given this suburb. They knew all their regular customers—not just their preferences in napkins, sheets and towels, but all about their families, their health, their holidays. They would listen to you, that was one of their greatest gifts. (Her husband tried not to smile.) Do you remember, Philip, the time I was ill with bronchitis—how they sent me flowers in hospital and cooked you some casseroles to tide you over? Now that's real manners, meaningful manners. And who's replacing them? *What's* replacing them? Yet another trendy boutique for female stick insects, with young assistants called Tallulah or Savannah or Rebel, who chew gum all day and, if our daughter is to be believed, assiduously avoid assisting you at all.'

Grace sighed again and took a sip of tea. Philip was beginning to look a little impatient, even mildly censorious, and she realised, blushing, that she'd gone too far. It was only last week that he'd chided her—gently of course, Philip was always the gentleman—for being so grumpy, so at odds with the world. He'd told her playfully that she was beginning to sound like a modern Miss Bates, albeit with more control over her syntax than Jane Austen's garrulous spinster. That her *idée fixe*, this constant talk of *bad manners among the young*, was becoming a little tiresome. He was right; she knew she shouldn't tar all young people with the same middle-aged brush. Her look and her words became more conciliatory.

'I know that life can be hard for young people these days,' she conceded, hoping to see her husband's smile of approval. 'Much harder than it was for us. Sometimes I think they must be drowning in choice. And they have to know so much more these days. I look at the size of their schoolbags and can see all the pressure they're under. Monica tells me that Jane is studying every night *and* weekends and feeling so stressed. It's all that competition for university places, she says, and now with those huge fees as well.'

Even as she spoke, gesturing towards moderation, her mind was heading back to the loud music that had shattered her sleep the night before—the assault of cacophonous drums and screeching voices and all that whining, wailing electric stuff.

'Mind you'—she began tapping on the table—'some of these students could use a lesson in manners. That couple two doors down from us, with their moronic music blasting away—they were at it again last night—thump thump, thump thump, thump thump, like some demented machine.'

Philip stood up from the table, released by the sound of the Number 9 bus in the distance.

'I'm off, love. Home at the usual time.'

'There's chicken casserole for dinner, darling. I'll see you at six.'

Grace lifted her face towards him for the ritual kiss. After twenty years of marriage, such habits were comforting. They confirmed both the stability of their relationship and the security of their world. Nevertheless, she felt a touch of self-reproach as she busied herself with the breakfast dishes; poor, forbearing Philip, she really must try not to talk so much, go on about the state of the world. It was time to get it out of her system, go for her daily walk to unclutter her mind, shut out the irritations of the morning, all the rudeness of the world. She always went the same way, through the leafy streets and then on to the park. Rosings was an established suburb, very quiet, very settled. Only a few rented places and a high proportion of professional people; a reassuring place really, clean and serene. Occasionally, it was true, a noisy motorbike or one of those bloody four-wheel drives (they drove Grace to a mild expletive) would roar past. But generally it was a pleasant walk, and the only people she encountered were usually known to her—fellow-walkers with whom she'd exchange a polite 'good morning', or by way of variation, some brief acknowledgement of the heat or the possibility of a shower.

As she set off briskly, Grace was relieved to see that her elderly neighbour Mrs Brown (calling her by her first name had never seemed an option) was not in her usual position, stationed dutifully in her immaculate front yard. The amount of water that woman wastes, Grace found herself thinking; morning and evening, soaking the foxgloves, snowdrops, forget-me-nots, in a stubborn replication of an English country garden. It was always best to hurry past the old lady's house, your eyes fixed on the ground. Grace had been caught up before by her neighbour's torrent of complaints about council rates, the noisy garbage trucks, how next door's jacaranda tree dropped leaves in her gutters. She occasionally glimpsed the old dear standing on her front verandah, surveying the neighbourhood, turning her face slowly, periscopically, from side to side, her expression a peculiar mix of generalised anxiety and smug self-righteousness. But this morning, thank goodness, Mrs Brown was nowhere in sight.

It was already quite hot as Grace set out. There were puddles of water on the footpath where pink-and-grey galahs gathered to drink, undisturbed by her passing footsteps. She admired their soft sheeny colours, the curve of their beaks as they bent their heads. The last holes of the golf course were dotted with players beating the heat. She could just make out a red hat in the distance and wondered if Jenny Anderson had started playing again after her operation. Grace felt a faint breeze brushing her face, heard the distinctive rise and fall of a kookaburra's laugh. She was in her stride now; soon she would be in that blank space she liked, that unbidden place, where she would feel calm and dreamily detached.

She was still in rather a haze as she left the park and moved onto the footpath, vaguely aware of the sun on her shoulders and a young girl walking towards her. Then, before she knew what was happening, bang! they collided. Not badly, but enough to make them both draw back with a start. Grace touched the girl's arm and smiled apologetically.

'I'm so sorry, I wasn't watching where I was going. You're not hurt, are you?'

To Grace's utter consternation, to her complete dismay, the girl snarled at her—*actually* bared her teeth—and then spat out *Fuckin' cow*, before giving her a bit of a shove, ever so light, but a shove nonetheless. Grace was dumbstruck and slightly shaken, as she watched the girl's receding figure stomping down the footpath—a large, waddling girl in very tight jeans, her head held high in the air. Vindicated. Solidified.

By the time Grace reached her street, she was feeling decidedly out of sorts. *Peeved*, Philip called her in this kind of mood. Here it was: further and incontrovertible proof of the incivility of the young. She had apologised, after all; what more was she supposed to do? Invite the girl home for a coca cola and a chat? Offer compensation? Images of screaming young hoons waving fists and fence pickets flashed into her mind. She pictured herself grabbing her phone and calling her daughter, her friend Marjorie, anyone—to unleash her anger, let off some steam. It was all so upsetting, so out of control. And then she saw Mrs Brown in her front garden, waving her hose in a cheery greeting, splashing water in profligate streams over flowers and footpath alike. Without stopping to think and still in a stew, still throbbing with muted rage, Grace waved in return and drew up in front of the old lady. Wanting sympathy, wanting vindication herself, on this most dreadful of mornings.

Mrs Brown smiled, all bright-eyed benevolence, at Grace's appearance.

'Hello, dear, been for your walk, have you? Getting hot already, good job you've got it over and done with.'

'Hello, Mrs Brown, how are you? Yes, it *is* hot today, it's going to be a scorcher.'

'You look all red in the face, dear. Are you alright?'

'Oh, it's nothing, Mrs Brown, really. I've just had a bit of an altercation with a young girl...Well, not an altercation exactly, but...' Grace found herself telling her tale, sanitised of course (*Fuckin' cow* became *Stupid cow*), but warming to her task, even impassioned, and ending with a self-justifying flourish, as she lamented *the lack of respect for older people these days, the general lack of good manners in the young.*

Mrs Brown chorused with alacrity:

'Oh, my dear, you are *so* right. Never a truer word. Do you know, just the other day, I was in the supermarket and I was struggling to reach a can from the top shelf and there was a young man who worked there standing right next to me and it was obvious that I couldn't reach, but do you think he would offer to help, no, I had to ask him direckly. And the look he gave me, you would have thought I'd asked him to carry my shopping to my car, not that they do that anymore these days, I had a good mind to report him to the manager. Yes, I couldn't agree with you more, dear, young people these days have no consideration for other people, roaring up the road in their noisy cars, leaning out of the windows shouting and raising their fists and playing their awful music everywhere, like that young couple next door to me, the din that comes out of their house every day, it's enough to make you go psychic, and I'm sure they're not even married. Not like the old days, young folk used to get married then and this used to be such a quiet suburb and children respected their elders, manners, they had, *please* and *thank you* and *I beg your pardon*, you don't hear that anymore these days.'

By now Mrs Brown was clutching Grace's arm with one hand, while the other continued to drown the delphiniums. Grace was startled by the tenacity of the old lady's grip as she registered her voice rattling on.

'Do you know, dear, I fully agree with that nice lady politician, you know the one who always looks so smart, so well-groomed, never a hair out of place, and that lovely smile she has, like a beacon of light, it is, you know the one who said that young people should be taught manners in school, learn how to use the correct silverware at the dinner table and how to break their bread rolls properly. Of course parents don't teach these kinds of things anymore, everyone's too busy and the mothers are all off at work these days, getting other people to bring up their children, half of them are *peedofeels*, you know, it's no wonder young people are so rude nowadays. And how terrible for you, you poor dear. Do come in and have a cup of tea.'

Despite some undeniable stirrings of irritation, Grace found herself soothed by her neighbour's kind invitation. It was a welcome balm after the shock of the recent incident—she could still see those bared teeth, feel that brutish shove, as though she, Grace Martin, were of no account at all. She even felt a little teary as she allowed herself to be steered by Mrs Brown's eager hand through the gate and over the threshold of her home.

'Do you know, dear,' continued the old lady, returning to her theme and beckoning Grace to a seat in the kitchen, 'I think most of the problem stems from a lack of discipline in those state schools. The teachers couldn't care less, they let them run amok, that's why so many parents are sending their children to private schools these days, they know what's good for them, I can tell you that children in *those* schools know how to break their bread rolls and which kind of knife and fork to use. Table manners, that's what this country needs. And discipline, they should go into the army, well, the boys anyway, do something useful with their lives, especially with this war on at the moment, do the right thing, I say, learn to respect authority. I strongly agree with our Prime Minister on this issue. Did you hear him on the telly the other day, talking about what's happened to manners in our society? The *decline* of good manners, he called it, such a good word, he always puts it so well.'

Grace nodded rather numbly as Mrs Brown fussed with cups and saucers. Seated in the darkness of the old woman's kitchen, with its disconcerting mix of mustiness and disinfectant, Grace was beginning to feel a lump of regret lodge painfully in her throat. Mrs Brown was on her way again.

'I always like to hear him talk, he always talks such common sense and he's always honest isn't he, what you see is what you get, and this particular speech, I must say, was no exception. He said that people shouldn't have to put up with bad manners or bad language, he said we should all start standing up for Australian values, whether we were born here or not, you come and live here, then you should live like us, he said, and I always say it too. Serves them right being put in those detention places, we didn't ask them to come here did we? And then the P.M., he went on to say that a lack of courtesy was increasing the amount of violence in our communities and how schools should concentrate on teaching manners and Shakespeare and that *what-the-Dickins* chappy, instead of all that politically correct business and teachers telling children to support the unions and which side to take in the war and all those sorts of things.'

Mrs Brown took a deep breath as she turned on the kettle. But she wasn't done yet, and there was little Grace could do to stop her, short of being rather rude.

'And you know, dear, the Prime Minister said that families need to get back to traditional Australian values, you know what he means, being mates and a fair go and owning your own house and saluting the flag at school every morning and saying prayers. Oh, and singing the national anthem, that was what that other nice pollie said, you know, the one who's always on the telly, the one who says women are having too many abortions, and I couldn't agree more. Anyway, he said it would be very rude not to play "God Save the Queen" when Her Majesty comes to open the Games, or was it the P.M. who said that? Well, whoever said it, it's right, all this Republican palaver, the Queen is such a wonderful lady, truly remarkable, she stayed in London during the Blitz, and she's always so polite to those dark chappies in Africa when it must be so hard for her. And the other thing this nice minister said was that when Her Majesty comes to Australia we should all sing "God Save the Queen" with enthusiasm, those were his exact words, it should be "sung enthusiastically", he said. He put it so well.' Mrs Brown looked for one ludicrous moment as though she was about to burst into an appropriately fervent rendition of the anthem, but instead she smiled, almost conspiratorially, at her neighbour. 'Don't you agree?'

Grace knew this was a rhetorical question and by now she was feeling dizzy and not a little alarmed. How could she extricate herself from this ludicrous babble, this maniacal word machine? It was almost comic, except for the fact, she suddenly realised with a start, that this disconcerting monologue of half-baked, prejudicial nonsense was so uncomfortably close to home. Mrs Brown, she saw with some dismay, was *herself* writ large, a cartoon Mrs Elton to her complacent Emma. Grace was overcome not only with the inanity, the idiocy, of her neighbour's oration but also by the shock of recognition. What, indeed, was going on in the world? Did it matter so much, after all, if a young girl had been rude to her in the street?

Mrs Brown called over her shoulder as she started making the tea.

'You've had a nasty shock, my dear, a nice cuppa and a piece of shortbread will be just the ticket.'

Now foolishly trapped by her own good manners, hearing the kettle wailing in sympathy with her plight, Grace had little choice but to wait it out. Patience is a virtue, she told herself. This too shall pass. As Mrs Brown dusted off her Royal Dalton cups and placed biscuits on a plate, Grace glanced at the newspaper on the table—the local tabloid, *The Clarion*, not one she ever read. She was aware of the old woman's continual nattering in the background as an annoying counterpoint to the boldness of the headline. 'Police Curb Violent Mob!' it trumpeted, in solid black two-inch font. Nothing like the exclamatory mode, Grace found herself thinking, to get the readers in. She skimmed the story about a protest at the Port Hedland Detention Centre. You didn't usually hear about these incidents—out of sight, out of mind, she knew—but this one, Grace remembered, had been rather spectacular, with police wielding batons, dragging the protestors by their hair. A photograph showed a young woman screaming at a policeman, and others milling about in the background. And still further away was a barbed-wire fence, barely discernible in shadowy grey. There were eyewitness accounts and the predictable comment from the Minister, warning the protestors *not to take the law into their own hands.* The law, the law; Grace found herself shaking her head. What kind of law, she wondered, was at work behind a barbed-wire fence?

Mrs Brown glanced over to the newspaper as she put the cups on the table and began pouring the tea. It must be her best china, thought Grace: such elegant white cups and saucers, with a fine gold line around the rims. A sharp voice broke into the momentary silence:

'Oh, I see you're looking at that picture of those dreadful young people, look at them, so scruffy and dirty, some of them look as though they haven't had a decent wash in months, and those ridiculous pants they wear, hanging halfway down their backsides—pardon my language, their derrieres. Look at them shaking their fists and there's one there in the corner, look, shouting at a policeman, so uncouth, it makes my blood boil, it does, and girls too, that's the worst of it, not a young lady in sight among that lot. And why are they wasting taxpayers' money doing these protest things, that's what I want to know, they should be learning to read and write. You know I heard on the telly the other day, it was that nice lady again, with the lovely yellow hair, so smooth and shiny, you can see *she* takes pride in her appearance, anyway she was saying that students don't even know how to read and write these days, they should be knuckling down to that instead of all this shouting and waving their fists and their bad language. They think they know everything but they don't even know where these people come from, they might jolly well have all sorts of diseases, like the—what was it—myxomatosis the Japs brought in after the war, or terrorists, they could be, those people with the funny things wrapped around their heads and those strange women with the long black dresses, you could hide a bomb under there, I heard some pollie saying the other day and it's true. Milk and sugar, dear?'

'No sugar. Just milk.'

Mind your Ps and Qs, Grace, she thought. 'Thank you,' she added, as Mrs Brown poured milk into her cup. She opened her mouth to say something, anything, to try to change the course of this mangled harangue. But Mrs Brown cantered off again, as she brushed biscuit crumbs from her mouth.

'It's the language, that's the worst of it. Those young people were on telly last night screaming and screaming at the police and shouting at the cameras, F this and F that, it was, truly shocking...'

As Mrs Brown took a sip of tea—even *she* couldn't talk and drink English Breakfast at the same time—Grace took the plunge.

'You know, Mrs Brown, sometimes young people become so angry about what they think is wrong, even if you don't agree with them, that they can't help using bad language. Or waving their fists. Or sometimes it's a way of drawing attention to a cause.'

Mrs Brown placed her teacup decisively on the saucer and held up her hand in admonition.

'That's all very well, dear, I certainly agree that it's a free country and people are allowed to say what they think, although heaven knows people think some very bad things these days, still, as I said, it's a free country, my Alf died in the war for that, you know, and I wrote a letter. But why do people have to speak so badly, all that swearing, it's all very upsetting, I couldn't begin to repeat it, it's so shocking and just so unnecessary. Like that young native on the news the other night who called our Prime Minister some words I simply couldn't repeat, he was on about the P.M. not saying sorry, all that business about being stolen from their families, you know how they go on about it, when of course it was for their own good, although you wouldn't know it, judging by the language this young fellow was using, I just couldn't bring myself to repeat it, especially that really nasty word, the one beginning with "c". It's disgraceful. They shouldn't be allowed to say such things.'

Grace was both astonished by this brief flirtation with brevity—Mrs Brown had managed to utter two short sentences consecutively—and appalled by her own passivity. Standing up from the table, she looked sternly at her neighbour and summoned up the courage to be frank. Her hands were trembling slightly but her voice was strong and clear.

'Do you know, Mrs Brown, that your manner of speech is disgraceful? Your syntax is convoluted, your structure illogical and your diction clichéd, repetitive and imprecise.'

Mrs Brown pointed her ear in Grace's direction. 'What was that, dear? You're not leaving already, are you?'

Grace remained composed. She was beginning to enjoy herself. 'Manner and matter are inseparable. When language is sloppy, thought is sloppy.'

Mrs Brown looked puzzled. 'What are you saying? I don't understand,' she piped.

Grace maintained her calm demeanour. 'I'm surprised you're taking the trouble to listen to me, Mrs Brown. Perhaps I should express myself more simply, more forthrightly, albeit, of course, most decorously. Heaven forbid—if you'll pardon a pompous metaphor—that I should stray from the paths of civility.'

Mrs Brown was perplexed. 'Are you feeing unwell, dear?' she asked.

Grace took a deep breath—it was such a deliciously decisive moment—and let Mrs Brown have it, once and for all.

'Mrs Brown, you have no capacity for rational thinking and argumentation. You lack the imagination to empathise with others less fortunate than yourself. You are a mindless, reactionary, self-righteous, snivelling racist; an elitist, xeno-phobic, jingoistic—*neighbour.*' (Grace hoped that the strong beat on which she'd ended her sentence would disguise her momentary loss of words.)

Mrs Brown was flustered, her teacup trembling in her hands.

'I don't understand what you're saying, but it doesn't sound very nice.'

'No indeed, Mrs Brown, it isn't nice at all. Just like you. Can I be plainer? Think of *me* as a rational creature speaking the truth from her heart.'

Grace took her leave with a mocking curtsey. She had made no difference, of course. Indeed, she felt certain that her polysyllabic smugness, her Austenian allusiveness, had actively prevented the ethical education to which her witless neighbour might be predisposed. And what about her *own* education, Grace asked herself, as she reflected on this comic-grotesque encounter with her diabolical double. As she walked out into the heat of the day, released from the kitchen torture of the morning, she told herself sternly to put her own house in order. She felt guilty, chastened and full of remorse. But also, she had to confess, undeniably good. Damn good, in fact; damn bloody good. Still flushed with the exhilaration of her measured vituperation, still buoyed by the memory of Mrs Brown's bewildered, stupid face, what else could she feel? Grace couldn't wait to tell Philip her story. Her narrative would be both contrite and condemnatory, and liberally spiced—she couldn't help smiling—with the strategic and ethical deployment of some carefully chosen, simply shocking and unspeakably ill-mannered words.

Such a shame

1. Get out of the water (1955)
When Nell was a little girl—she couldn't have been more than five or six—her family used to go for picnics out of town, often with her Auntie May, Uncle Herb and the cousins. They always went to the same spot and she loved it there, because you saw birds of different colours, sometimes even a kangaroo, and because her mum always packed a nice lunch. Nell liked to help her mum spread the picnic blanket on the ground, avoiding any ant holes; best of all was taking the food out of the basket and setting it out neatly, with the plates, knives and forks. It made her feel grown up. She and her cousins used to swim in the lake; the water was clear and clean, very blue. Nell had only just learnt to swim small distances, but she could dog paddle for a long time and keep herself afloat by lying on her back.

One time she stayed in the water for ages. Her cousins had given up swimming and gone for ice creams. Nell knew that her mum and dad were keeping an eye on her, making sure she didn't go out too far. She was lying on her back when she heard a bright voice say hello to her, and she saw a girl with a friendly face and a big wide smile pop up next to her in the water. Nell had never seen this girl before and they started talking about where they went to school and what they liked, and the girl showed Nell how she could do two different kinds of strokes, breaststroke as well as over-arm. She said her name was Sadie. Nell thought Sadie was very clever, and she liked her happy face and big white teeth.

Just then she heard people calling out her name and she saw her dad waving for her to get out of the water. Nell thought she must have drifted out a bit too far, or maybe everyone was packing up to go home. She said goodbye to Sadie, who waved wildly at her, saying *Goodbye, goodbye, goodbye*, and laughing. Nell hurried out of the water, into the arms of her dad. He had a really red face, it was his cross face, and he bent right down to look at her, snarling, *I don't want you talking to those Abos, do you understand? They're dirty.* Nell didn't understand at all, and when she looked back at the lake, she could see that Sadie was still in the water, still waving at her.

2. Country town (1968)

Gerry grew up in a country town, where it was always hot and dusty. He didn't care that there were always black kids in his class. Some years there were one or two, other years a lot more. Some of his friends called them boongs and niggers, but the black kids didn't seem to mind. It seemed almost friendly, and anyway, they all played footy together at school and bashed each other up for fun. His mum had told him that *boong* and *nigger* were rude words; *they're natives, that's their proper name*, she'd said.

In Grade 5, Gerry made friends with a native girl called Maud, who was new in town and really good at gymnastics. She'd twirl around on the high beam and she could do great cartwheels. Maud would turn wheel after wheel after wheel until you couldn't see her anymore and you'd have to run after her. One day Gerry asked his mum if he could bring Maud home to play, but his mum said natives were to be *tolerated*—that was the big word she used—*not for bringing home. You must keep your distance, Gerald*, she told him.

3. Burglary (1980)

Lena is terrified that night. She wakes up because she's heard something, and when she sits up in bed she sees a shape, a man's dark shape, standing at the door. She's bolt upright, frozen, the thought pounding in her head, *This is the end, this is the end, he's going to kill us*. But the man turns and walks away, quickly, down the hall. Lena shakes her husband as lightly as she can and tells him what's happened. They both lie immobilised, feeling the pulsing of their bodies and listening for unfamiliar noises. Eventually, after who knows how long, Bob gets out of bed, very carefully, and Lena follows closely, hanging on to his pyjamas. They creep around each corner of the house, looking for the intruder they hope like hell they won't find. Then they see the shattered front window, glass strewn everywhere, and Lena becomes even more frightened while Bob tries to stay calm. They ring the police, who come round an hour later, at three in the morning. Nothing seems to have been stolen, but Lena can't stop shaking as she drinks her cup of tea.

Later that morning the neighbours who'd seen the police car in the driveway come round to find out what happened. As soon as Lena tells them her story—she can still see the shape in the doorway—the neighbours nod in understanding and ask if it was an Aborigine. She tells this story several times over the next few days, and each time, she's asked the same question. At some point—it's difficult to say exactly when—the dark shape in

Lena's narrative becomes an armed Aborigine wanting money for drugs. The black man who scared the life out of them.

4. Saturday in Freo (1998)

Jake often takes the train to Fremantle on a Saturday, just to walk around, take in the atmosphere. It's so much livelier than Perth. You always see interesting people in Freo, eccentric people—like the woman with the long purple cloak and the orange feathers in her hair, who sings loudly as she walks, songs like 'Mamma', in a harmless kind of way. Jake likes to sit for hours in the cappuccino strip, listening to the buskers and checking out the girls, reading the paper, talking to the locals. Sometimes he and his mates go to the park and have a game of bocce with the Italian blokes, or play darts with the Irish drunks in the pub. Feeling the sun on your face, just doing nothing much, is a good way to spend an afternoon.

There's one place he avoids and that's the mall where the blacks hang out. Jake doesn't think he's a racist, it's just that he gets upset by their drunken pushing and shoving, the abusive screaming. He hasn't walked through the mall since the day he was threatened with a broken bottle and had to run away. Shit scared he was. But what upset him most were the reactions of the people looking at the Aborigines—indignant, disgusted, giving the blacks a wide berth. You can't blame them, Jake thinks, but still he hated the way they kept turning round to have another look. Jake doesn't know what he can do about it really, any of it, so he just doesn't go to the mall anymore.

5. Children's Law Court (2005)

Neal is accompanying his widowed aunt to the Children's Law Court. She's been called as a witness to a street bashing, in which an elderly man was knocked down by two youths who stole his wallet. Despite his aunt's horror at what happened—it could easily have been her they assaulted—she was able to give the police a detailed description of the two and the licence plate of their car. The alleged offenders, boys really, thirteen or fourteen years old, are now being brought to trial. Neal knows that his aunt is nervous—she keeps scrunching up her handkerchief and making funny noises in her throat—as she sits with four other witnesses in a spacious room surrounded entirely by glass walls. She's anxious because she's never been in a courtroom before and because she can be seen by the Aboriginal youths and their large family, who are waiting in the well-lit lobby, sitting quietly, saying very little. Neal imagines what his aunt is thinking: She's a kind woman with liberal inclinations, but he can see the fear in her eyes. She's thinking, *they can see me, they know who I am, they can find out where I live and break down my door.*

Neal sees the witnesses watching the family all the time, trying not to look, but looking all the same. As they wait, they exchange their eyewitness accounts, their narratives of that dreadful day. They relive each moment, all the grisly, arousing details—the punches, the blood, the old man's screams as he fell to the ground. When stories about the case are exhausted, one of the witnesses adds another one, about how his petrol station was held up last year by *a gang of Abos.*

The garage owner points his head in the direction of the Aboriginal family and says with pinched lips:

'Look at the lot of 'em. No wonder they get into trouble, they have way too many kids, if you ask me.'

Neal is surprised and heartened by his aunt's composed protest: 'But look at how well dressed they all are. Very neat, very clean. The children are obviously well looked after.'

The garage owner looks put out by this objection, but because he is polite to elderly women, he doesn't raise his voice:

'Call that lookin' after your kids, when they let 'em roam the streets at all hours, bashin' an old man, poor bugger, he was so shook up. And in any case, they're only turnin' it on because they have to show up in court, impress the judge by lookin' all clean and tidy. Most of the time they run around in rags, their noses aren't even wiped, some of 'em.'

The young man in the shiny brown suit says pompously, 'And they probably borrowed those clothes from some charity organisation, which we pay for, do we not?'

'All that welfare, it doesn't do them any good at all', adds the middle-aged woman with carefully coiffed, flaming-red hair. She speaks with the clipped tones of self-righteous certitude. The garage owner is pleased, because he can see by the looks on people's faces that most of them are on his side.

Neal begins to feel clammy; he loosens his tie. The room in which they sit is huge and high-ceilinged, but he feels out of breath, as though he's sitting inside a big glass bubble, airless and close. He can tell that his aunt is upset and he takes her hand, wanting her to know that he shares her feelings. It's taken less than ten minutes for these speeches, these set pieces, to emerge.

The family in the lobby is becoming restless, too. The two boys are moving from foot to foot and then pacing a little. A white woman, a court official in uniform, hovers around them, occasionally talking to them. The mother begins to laugh at something, and the witnesses voice their indignation at her obvious lack of remorse. Then, one of the children, a girl of about three or four, escapes from the mother's lap and runs over to where the witnesses are sitting. She stares at them, all eyes, through the glass walls. They stare back at her, a tiny, pitch-black little girl with tight plaits, dressed in a pale blue pinafore. She is doll-like, enchanting, with her dark skin and black eyes, and they can't help but watch her as she begins to dance, twirling round and round, holding out her little dress, standing on her toes. It's a thoroughly winsome performance.

The red-haired woman has been smiling. But then, as the little girl winds down her dance and sticks out her tongue in mischievous merriment, she frowns and sighs, 'They're so beautiful at that age. It's such a shame they can't stay that way. They go off the rails so young, don't they?'

Neal takes his aunt's hand again, as they sit waiting in silence to be called in for the trial.

The monstrous arc

It's already ten in the morning and still she hasn't showered and dressed for the day ahead. Dishes from last night's dinner are heaped in the sink and teetering on the kitchen bench, rebuking her. She tries not to look because the brown blurs of food on the plates remind her of the cockroach streaks she finds in cupboards and which she's too disgusted to wipe away. Thomas is having one of his clinging mornings, tugging at her pyjama pants, grasping her leg to stop her walking past. He's howling with that siren wail she hates, that winds up and up, more and more shrilly, whenever she turns away from him. When she relents and picks him up, he gropes clumsily at her breasts like a stupid adolescent boy, all fumbles and eager nuzzlings, as though she's nothing but this pair of jelly mounds disconnected from the rest of whoever she is. She stopped feeding him months ago, for goodness sake, but still he demands, assails her, sniffs her out. When will this end, Charlie thinks. When will she be done with this draining, this obliterating, life of the body? What happened to that picture she once had in her head: her Laura Ashley fantasy, sitting in a wicker chair reading a book, the sunlight streaming onto her paisley dress, her angel-baby in a carrycot, sleeping at her feet.

She removes her son's grubby hands from the folds of her pyjama shirt. When he persists, kneading her with sticky, greedy fingers, she dumps him on the floor, harder than she'd intended, and gives him a smack on the leg.

'Stop it, Thomas, stop assaulting me!' Charlie doesn't care that he won't understand what she's saying, the *assaulting* part at least. *Stop* is pretty clear though, as sharp as the edge to her voice. But *assaulting* will mean nothing, she knows, to this two-year-old boy, stuck in his amoral, worm-blind world. Charlie thinks of the time she spent talking to him as a baby, bathing him in language, as the gurus decreed. As she fed him, wiped the yoghurt from his face, with his chubby-chop cheeks so deliciously soft, she would name the objects and the movements—*silver spoon, fleecy flannel, clean and whisk away*; every mealtime a crafted lesson. Even when changing his nappies, she would happily chatter to her oblivious son. *What a wondrous boy you are, sweet Thomas. Your tummy was made for tickling.* She remembers the time he peed in her face as he lay, magisterially indifferent, on the change-table. *What a beauty, Thomas!* she'd exclaimed, laughing at the shock. *What a magnificent arc!*

She hears him crying and remembers that she's just smacked him, not hard of course, it's never hard. She opens her pyjama shirt wearily and picks him up again, letting him pat her breasts and squeeze them, squealing and gurgling, throwing back his head in brazen delight. Thomas has few words and he uses them sparingly, deliberately so, perhaps, in this battle of wills on which they seem to have embarked and in which she feels more and more defeated, almost, on some days, lost. *No. Me want. More. Mine.* Imperatives, possessives, defiant monosyllables. Relentless and impenetrable. Now that he is, for the moment, satisfied, Thomas wriggles out of her arms and scampers, a happy monkey on all fours, to his toybox. Charlie watches him arranging his action figures, his body upright with earnest concentration, and then suddenly launching them across the room, roaring as they thump on the tiles and then against the wall. She's already too tired to chastise him. She's always tired these days. Her clinic sister, with indefatigable cheeriness, told her that a sense of humour was *crucial for keeping your sanity, dear. Laugh or else you'll cry.* As she stands there, watching her child burbling to his toys, Charlie remembers the smack and remembers too, not for the first time, what her mother told her not long before Thomas was born. A rare moment of confessional intimacy. *Sometimes,* her mother had whispered, looking over her shoulder, *I would get so mad at you that I would have to leave the room and shut the door. I knew if I started to hit you I would break every bone in your body.*

Now that Thomas is distracted, Charlie heads for the bathroom, picking up a toy and throwing it back into the box. It was all so much easier when he couldn't walk. He didn't sleep much, but at least she could pin him down, put him in his cot and close the door, try to ignore the cries of abandonment as she washed the dishes, went to the toilet, hung out the nappies. Charlie remembers standing back from the clothesline and surveying the rows of clean white cloth, hearing a plane overhead, looking up at the sky and seeing nothing but the roofs of other houses, neighbours' houses, houses in the street beyond, strangers everywhere. She said to herself, *This is what my life has become*: nappies flapping in the wind, rows and rows of terracotta, and a plane she couldn't see. She remembers laughing grimly. Still, Thomas was stationary then, and she could get things done, get herself fixed up. The smartly dressed, made-up young mum, walking Thomas in the city in his pram, pathetically grateful when strangers ooed and aahed over her adorable baby. He *was* beautiful; everyone could see it.

She remembers the first time she saw him. It was a caesarean birth, an emergency, and just before she went under, just before they put her out, she felt both woozy and sad, an abject, doped-up failure. She remembers a last-minute, panicky stab of thought, that her medical problems were self-induced, a cowardly and contemptible evasion of the pain of giving birth. And then she's waking up and someone is putting him in her arms, her baby, swaddled so tightly that only his tiny head is visible. She gasps at his beauty: the alabaster smoothness of his skin, the delicate forehead, the midnight blue of his father's eyes looking up at her, into her. The feel of him, so warm, so small, so yielding; the smell of his newness. She can't stop looking at him. When a nurse places him in his cot, Charlie holds out her arms and begs to have him returned to her, to the safety of her bed, her body. Such seriousness, she thinks now, such foolishness, about a baby.

She can hear Thomas kicking up a fuss again and knows she'll have to put him in his playpen—*a pen for a little piggie*, she used to tease him—to have any chance of a shower. Electrical appliances, falling crockery, sharp knives; there's danger every-where. So it's done, with the usual protests and a quick scramble to the shower. She'd give anything to linger under the warm streams of water, letting them run down her sloping body, like a lover's undemanding caress. Her most precious indulgence is the weekend shower when his father takes Thomas for a walk or plays games with him, when she can stand there for as long as she likes, letting the water run, letting it fall and fall, herself dissolving. It's the best feeling in the world. But today is Wednesday, she tells herself, as she dries off hurriedly, and Adam will be gone for the rest of the week. Sometimes she would like to tell him how she feels, about the times he goes away, even for a few days, about her tiredness, her anger, her boredom, her sadness, a mess of emotions, like a room littered with toys and washing, a desk piled with unpaid bills, such a mess she doesn't know where to start. She would like to tell him but she can't because she knows she's weak and he is strong, uncomplaining, as straight and uncomplicated as an arrow, while she is knotted up and miserable, with no one to blame. She would like to tell him all of this, some of this, but she can't. He'll have to make it up to me when he comes home, she tries to smile to herself, unable to imagine what *make it up* might mean.

'Oh stop it, Thomas, I'm coming,' she mumbles as she re-appears before him. He's not shaking the playpen as usual but now he's beginning to whinge. It's the whinging, so unreasonable, so childish, that really gets to her. She stoops and scoops him up, reluctantly, resigned to half-an-hour of grumbling before he's given a quick wipe with the flannel, changed and dressed for their walk to the park. Wednesday morning is always park morning and some part of her swears that Thomas knows this already, so that the slightest deviation from his comfortable routine makes him restless, on his guard. She brushes back the curls from his sweaty forehead and wonders if he's running a temperature. He snakes his arms around her body and she thinks of the day, a few years ago it was, when Laura turned up at her door with a clinging baby in her arms. Charlie can still see the boldness of the sky, the shock of light, behind the woman in the doorway. There she was—Laura, tall and golden, in a red caftan with mirrors, a radiant apparition in the suburbs. With a baby. Six months old? Nine months? Charlie couldn't tell. This one seemed startled, her pudgy arms clutching at her mother's neck. Laura: this hippie, beaded woman from the past, standing there with a fat-faced, red-faced baby, slung almost insolently on her hip.

'Charlotte! Hey!' She smiled warmly. Charlie remembered that smile: winning, people called it. Always ready to help out, was Laura. A good egg, they called her at school.

'Well, ask me in, why don't you?'

'Laura. What...what are *you* doing here?'

Charlie let her in and shut out the morning light, worried that her words had been impolite, wondering what she could, or might, say next. But there was no time to speak, as Laura unfurled the baby, unceremoniously, from her body and dumped her on the floor. She stood up and made a loud *harrumphing* noise.

'Can you take this child off my hands for a bit? I can't stand her touching me anymore.'

Charlie was shocked and turned around to look, relieved that no one else was there. She recalls two pictures from that morning: a baby who cried as she tried to bounce her up and down, and Laura, glimpsed through the kitchen window, walking around the garden, looking up at the trees. She hasn't seen her, or the baby, since, and she's heard that she's pregnant again. Whether by accident or design Charlie doesn't know.

They set off for the park. Thomas is quiet now, and still, strapped in his pusher. *Take them outside when it gets too much*, her mother had told her, before leaving for her holiday overseas. *They love watching the birds and feeling the wind on their face.* Charlie had agreed with the advice but flinched at the idea of 'them' and 'they'. Funny, she thinks, how quickly people start asking when you're going to *have a second*. Even when she was in the hospital bed, waiting tearily for her milk to come in, a relative she hadn't seen for years popped up to coo and beam and dispense advice, to pronounce that *the sooner you have another one, the better. Only children are very selfish, you know.*

Charlie's breathing is easier now. She's trying to do what the clinic sister told her, *enjoy the good times, don't dwell on the bad.* The sister has four children of her own, all grown up, so she knows what she's talking about. But already Charlie is thinking of the night ahead, the broken sleep, the wretched greyness of those interminable hours, the getting up, the falling into sleep again, the bliss of it, and then hearing another cry, as if she hadn't slept at all, and then getting up again. A zombie in a twilight zone. This sleeplessness, this unrelenting madness, recall to her another friend, steady, reliable Jean, who'd moved a few years ago to another city. A scientist, rational and methodical, who'd planned the conception and birth of her baby with the arithmetical precision for which she was renowned. But when her daughter arrived, Jean was lifted up, carried away, by the joyous unexpectedness of it all. She called the child Dora. *It means 'gift',* she'd gushed in a letter. *She's the best one I've ever had.* Another time Jean had phoned, all whispery, to describe how she would tiptoe into Dora's room at night, to watch her sleeping, to listen to her snuffly noises, *just to make sure she's still alive.* What had happened to this woman, to phlegmatic, no-nonsense Jean, to be so enthralled by a baby, to be held captive in this way? It was then, Charlie thinks—Jean's besotted letters, her enraptured words—that she must have started thinking about having one of her own. Adam had been making noises for a while, nothing too heavy, dropping into the conversation stories about a colleague's new baby, *Des brought her into the office yesterday, as cute as pie she was.* Her curiosity must have been aroused, something must have changed, and somehow, without really talking about it, without really thinking about it, she'd found herself pregnant. Perhaps, she thinks now, curiosity is as good a reason as any.

But it was then too, Charlie remembers, that she'd lost touch with Jean. She didn't hear from her for months. She didn't give it too much thought, her mind on other things. The colour of the nursery. All the new equipment to be bought: Charlie had no idea babies required so much. And then a letter came, with no lyrical phrases, no praises, no miraculous transformations. The handwriting was microscopic, cramped-up, as though the words were hiding, ashamed of themselves. A pitiable narrative of the weeks of sleepless nights, fretful days, how one night she'd gone in to the crying baby, this precious gift, and picked her up and tried to calm her, tried everything for hours on end, but nothing had worked, and then she said she *just snapped*, she just wanted to throw her baby against the wall, shut it up, shut it up, just smash it up for good and all. *I came so close, Charlie*, she wrote. She'd been holding the baby in her arms and had wanted to throw her against the wall. She signed off, *I am a monster.* She didn't write her name. Charlie remembers calling and trying to console and reassure. Holding the phone with one hand, with the other smoothing her proud, her smug, pregnant belly; trying to keep the edge of disapproval from her voice. Perhaps Jean had heard it; in any case she hasn't been in touch again. Charlie would like to talk to her, to tell her what she knows, now, but perhaps, she thinks, the time has passed.

Thomas's shouting breaks her reverie. She bends to unstrap him from the pusher, this solid, determined boy-child who rolls over on the ground in his hurry to be free. He heads off straightaway for the puddles made by council sprinklers but Charlie is already primed for this scenario, the same for several weeks in a row. This mania for repetition, she laments, flying after him. Doesn't he ever get bored with this game, for this is how she sees it, this daily tussle between mother and child. She pictures his father on the plane, on his way to Sydney, *back before you know it*, he'd said, smothering his son with kisses on his tummy and squeezing Charlie on the arm before rushing out the door, late as always. A good man, a helpful man, a very busy man. *Little shit*, Charlie thinks as she sees Thomas jump in the puddles and turn to grin at her. So what does it matter if his shoes get wet, his clothes? She's slowing down now, thinking he can just get wet, splash himself as much as he likes, she just doesn't care. Thomas, she sees, is looking perplexed, his face turned up at her, waiting for a cue. He doesn't know what to do, she thinks, this isn't part of the game, or it's a new game he doesn't know. Charlie feels glad, stupidly glad.

Bored now with waiting, Thomas takes off, arms flapping, to the slides and plonks himself at the foot of the ladder. Charlie can see his feet stomping in the distance and hear his impatient cry. He doesn't call her name; he rarely calls her *Mumma* or *Mum-mum* or any of the words he's supposed to say. She doesn't know whether this should be a matter of concern. She makes her way to the slide, her hands in the pockets of her jacket, taking her time, for she has all the time in the world. Thomas is hollering now, no words, just this solipsistic bellow of command, his sturdy legs still marching up and down. There's no one else in the park this morning; it is entirely his. Without speaking, Charlie helps him up the ladder. He's eager to climb, his legs a tangle of furious intent, and when he gets to the top, he wriggles out of her grasp and shoots down the slide, released and triumphant, squealing as he goes. He has no fear, Charlie thinks. He demands another lift up the ladder, another slide, another, five times over, ten. She wants to stop this bending and hoisting and lifting, this mindless movement back and forth, a puppet on a string. She's had enough and moves to go, beckoning Thomas to follow her as she makes her way from the slide. He hollers again and runs after her, pulling at her jeans, and when Charlie bends down to him, poised to complain, he puffs up his trembling lips and spits in her face. Cold and hard and ugly, like a slap. She can feel it, a humiliating glob, sticky on her cheek. It's the worst feeling in the world.

As she wipes the spittle from her face, the melody of the Mr Whippy van sounds in the distance, as tinny and wearied and metallic as her heart. Thomas is all agog, pointing and tugging again at her jeans, shouting one of the few nouns he knows, or shows. *I-cream*, he shrills, *i-cream*, *i-cream*, and then louder still when Charlie stands her ground. She hears his puny tyranny, his maddening, high-pitched, feeble voice, competing with the gusting wind, a lawnmower's doleful moan, the roar of passing cars: all the weight of the world with which he must contend. She feels her spirits rise as she glowers over him. *I said no, Thomas. No ice cream today.* Incontestable, unaccountable. Thomas is enraged, his fists beating her thighs, drumming madly, ineffectually. He begins to scream, kicking her feet, his tiny leather boots making spiteful divots in the ground. *I-cream*, *i-cream*, he cries. Charlie picks him up, hauls him upside down and marches to the swing. She is confident and strong, her face burning fiercely against the morning cold. She dumps him roughly, with intent, onto the seat of the swing. She knows what will happen as she pushes, faster, higher, all her body weight behind the swing, her breathing deep and hard. She knows that the swing will wind up and up, almost out of sight. She knows that the child will scream in terror as his tiny body flies through the air in a monstrous arc. She knows all this and knows that she must stop.

Put on your dancing shoes

My husband always said that one could judge a person's character by their table manners when they ate alone. That, and the state of their footwear. In his view, shoes which were scuffed and down-at-heel signified, not mere scruffiness or even bohemian raffishness, and certainly not poverty or deprivation. No, for him, such shoes revealed a profound moral torpor on the part of their owner. A lack of self-discipline and self-respect, a disturbing disregard for keeping up appearances. Similarly, to eat alone in a boorish or piggish manner was for him incontrovertible proof of evolutionary regression. To slurp, to gobble, to stuff, to slop, was like going native, going troppo, in the genteel suburbs of Melbourne. It was akin to entering a heart of darkness. My husband was serious, he was firm, about such matters.

You think I exaggerate: you think my mode satiric, my language hyperbolic. You may be right. But I simply wished to convey to you some sense of the hell into which I descended in my fifty years of marriage—fifty years of moral pedagogy, an abyss of propriety and respectability, of atrophy and stupefaction. You can hear the mockery in my voice, my tone of amused contempt. But let me be clear: it was no laughing matter.

It was murder, I tell you, bloody murder. And now I am free. At seventy years of age, I have flown the coop, raised the rafters, all hell has been let loose. I am, at last, liberated and alive!

Oh, I know what you're thinking. She's murdered her husband. What a cheap trick, I hear you protesting, a creaky and transparent narrative ruse, the clumsy use of a Freudian slip. But you'd be wrong to think this. I am free, yes, released from the prison of propriety, the catacomb of loveless despair, but not through an act of homicide or manslaughter, murder in the first or third degree. Not that I haven't thought about it, mind you. And if you're honest with yourself, you'll confess that you've thought about it too. We all have dark places in the heart to which we mustn't go, forbidden, treacherous, unthinkable places. Who hasn't fantasised about the death of someone close to them, someone we're supposed to love? The opportunistic, unscrupulous Becky Sharp willed it, of course, and even that paragon of virtue, the endlessly self-sacrificing Dorothea Brooke, had a moment when she wished her sexless, self-pitying, arid and egotistical husband would simply snuff it. You dream of an act of fate, an act of God, an accident...And then you lie awake at night, listening for the sound of the car pulling up in the driveway, and it doesn't, and an hour passes, two hours, and you begin to feel panicky, then guilty, because what you wished for might have come true. The person is dead on the highway, mangled and bloody, it's unspeakable, you didn't really mean for this to happen. You wait for the policeman's knock on the door, his sombre face, the bad news...But wait, I seem to have run away with myself. What was I saying? Ah yes, my loveless marriage, a catacomb of despair.

Where do I begin, how should I begin to tell you? How can I describe the husbandly horrors to which I was subjected? The wedding night should have told me something. I should have been warned when Hugo insisted that I bathe, not once, but twice, before we made love. Even as a blushing bride, I knew instinctively this wasn't right. I must admit, however, that in the early days my husband was quite a proficient lover, if proficiency is what you're after. For a man of his generation, he was, sexually speaking, remarkably considerate. He always demanded my satisfaction and, to achieve this end, must have calculated early in our marriage the number of strokes it required for me to reach a climax (I was nothing if not compliant). Impeccable timing, Hugo had; never a moment too soon or too late. He must have been counting in his head, one, two, three, four, five, and so on, until the job was done. Not to mention the cleaning up afterwards. No sheet was left unturned in the search for a rebellious stain. It was all so mechanical, so dutiful, and in the end, so tiresomely predictable. You think it astonishing that a man of the fifties would have contemplated the sexual needs of his wife. I'll concede this point. Nevertheless, my needs were not, were never, the same as my desires, and therein lay the problem. One night when I cried out with pleasure, my husband, ever so politely, put his hand over my mouth. *Felicity*, he whispered reprovingly, *some moderation, if you please. Don't let your feelings run away with you.* There were many times when I wanted my feelings to run away with me, but I didn't know where they, or I, could go.

Pass over a few years and consider the issue of children. I had always wanted them, had always assumed that my husband and I would be in compete agreement on this matter. Wasn't it natural, I asked myself, for a man to want the continuation of his name, his line? Wasn't it natural for a woman to wish to nurture, guide, envelop with love? But Hugo made it perfectly clear, a few years after we were married, that children were a hindrance, an obstacle, a nuisance. A hindrance or an obstacle to *what* I was never quite sure. But there was no doubt that my husband considered children a physical inconvenience. They were messy and dirty, he intoned. Their noses ran, they dribbled their food, they vomited, urinated and defecated in the most inappropriate of places. Even when they were older, he declared, they made their physical presence evident in the most repellent and odious ways. What choice did I have but to submit to his wishes, to pretend to see the world through his antiseptic, joyless eyes? What choice did I have but to feel the emptiness of my arms, my breasts, my heart?

Let's move on to the sixties—the swinging sixties I believe they were called—although for me they were as calcified as the preceding decade of my marriage. My husband saw the bright mini skirts of the young girls in the street and I heard his clucks of disapproval. *Tut tut*, he tut tutted, clicking his tongue like a clock, *this is a travesty of femininity*. (As you can see, Hugo was a highly articulate man, and, before he died, living proof that linguistic facility is no guarantee of rationality or moral flexibility.) It was the moving flesh that seemed to trouble him, all that rippling of legs and the hint of jiggling buttocks. He wanted bodies, including his own, to be straitjacket-still, upright, controlled. It was the same with music. *How can they call this music?* He shook his head in that way he had, slowly moving it from side to side several times, looking so grave and so grey. *This caterwauling, this screaming, these moans and groans.* I suggested listening more carefully, listening to the words: the first kiss, lazy Sunday afternoons, a girl who was a man called Lola, quitting your job, revolution. *Why should I bother*, he droned. *It's all nonsense.* I tried to argue that it was all about movement, *it makes you want to move*, I said. Hugo had no idea what I was talking about.

Perhaps I should apologise if this version of my husband seems like a caricature of a human being. Implausible, unbelievable, unrealistic, I hear you say. Unjust, unkind, a ludicrous simplification of the complexity that characterises every human being. Well, yes and no. I have failed, I know, to endow him with the inner life to which he is entitled and which I must presume he possessed. I have, I concede, created an automaton. Yet I do believe this represents the essence of the man: his irreducible rigidity, his emotional fixity, his barely-aliveness. My construction may not seem real but it is, I contend, indisputably true.

Let me tell you about the way he danced, or failed to dance. What follows is exemplary and, I hope, instructive. I have always been drawn to the pleasures of dancing, even in the days when it was considered unseemly for a woman to show her legs, shake her hips, move with the slightest hint of abandon. I loved the sense of exhilaration, the whirling and twirling, the looping and strutting, my skirt swirling round me, the breathlessness of it all. Or the quieter movements, the slow, sensuous dip and glide, my dress clinging to my body like a second skin. Of course I only danced like this in my head. Indeed, I rarely danced in the flesh throughout my entire married life, because my husband made it clear that he wanted no part in moving about to music, no gyrating, no twisting, no quick steps or tangos, no fox trots or cha cha chas. He said it once, just before our bridal waltz, and he never said it again.

Now I have often heard wifely laments about their husbands' disinclination or inability to dance. *Fred has two left feet*, they complain. *Norm just won't get up on the dance floor, no matter how much I beg and plead. Merv is hopeless, he has no sense of rhythm at all. That's men for you,* they say, *what else can you expect?* Such are the jocular, indulgent remarks of disappointed wives. But my husband's refusal to dance was of another order altogether. Our wedding reception said it all. Hugo hoisted me up under my arms, his body stiff with rectitude. He looked me in the eye and said, firmly, *This is our first and only dance, Felicity. I have no choice at this moment, but be in no doubt that I won't be doing it again.* So we danced that night, with decorum and propriety. We danced apart, sedately, silently, one two three, one two three, one two three. My husband's rigid body was the only explanation I ever received, or required.

During the seventies, Hugo's rigormortised approach to life took another, and even more ludicrous, turn. He began to develop a decided aversion to the sight of my body hair. I first noticed this on the day he chastised me for leaving hair in the bathroom sink. Since it was unclear to whom the strands belonged, I assumed I was guilty of nothing more than a minor domestic transgression. The next morning, however, when Hugo emerged from the bathroom in a red-faced flutter, I knew something else, something far more serious, was at stake. *Felicity,* he declared, his nostrils flaring, *I have discovered a piece of your pubic hair in the soap. Don't let this happen again.* I didn't know whether to laugh or feel alarmed. His sense of repugnance was even more pronounced the next evening, when he was ready to perform his conjugal duty (by now reduced to once a month and always on a Friday night, at the end of his working week). Ruskin-repelled by the sight of my pubic hair, Hugo simply turned away and left the bedroom in dignified haste. This was the last time we made love, if that's what you want to call it. I'm sure that learned people have invented a name for this kind of condition, but all I knew was that I wanted to escape. But it was the eighties, I was fifty, and I felt I had little room to move.

And so we simply kept on going. Hugo and I were nearing our seventies. While I managed to retain a spring in my step, he limped and shuffled his way into the new century. The naughties, people were calling it, but as you can imagine, there was nothing naughty about the state of our union. Oh, I know that the thought of the elderly having sex is for many people unutterably obscene. They think that copulation between old people, like the violent scenes in a Greek tragedy, should take place off-stage, out of sight. *Abskene*, as it were. You know it is happening, but you would rather not see it, thank you very much. I do not subscribe to this view at all. Quite the opposite, in fact. I wanted to see it, but it just wasn't happening. But let me be clear: what I felt cannot be reduced to mere sexual frustration. It was much more than this, more profound, altogether more anguishing. Have you ever felt like your body wasn't there? That you are a phantom, a ghost, a disembodied consciousness, doomed forever to hover over a world you can see below you, where people laugh, touch, eat heartily, make love, walk and run, tickle and stroke and wrap their arms around one another, and dance, dance in the daytime, dance the night away, dance all the time, because the music inside you never dies. That is how I felt, more and more, like a missing person, until I almost began to forget what it was I was missing.

And then I was thrown a lifeline, I was flattened by a benevolent bolt of lightning, floored, had my socks knocked off. Let me tell you how it happened, this miracle of mine. I was doing what I always did on a Monday morning: returning from the local shops with a small bag of groceries: a carton of milk, a loaf of bread and two ripe bananas, one for Hugo, one for me. (Once I ate both bananas in one day, simply to get a reaction. I was hoping for a moral lecture, which at least would confirm that my husband was alive. And it would give me a laugh of sorts.) I heard the usual music blaring out of the loudspeakers from the public swimming pool—Monday morning was always aqua-aerobics for the over sixties—and the tune was lively, bump-and-grind, upbeat. Just the shot for a group of elderly ladies wanting to get fit, or keep the arthritis at bay.

Ahead of me on the footpath were three men, sweeping and raking the leaves. They were council workers dressed in black shorts, logoed shirts and hats. I had never seen them here before. All of them in their sixties, I estimated, all wiry and grey-haired, with those comically skinny legs that men, even the portlier ones, often acquire in their autumn years. As the music continued to pump away, as the men continued to sweep and rake, I saw one of them begin to dance. While the other two kept on with the job, this one took his broom, shook it about, moved his hips, gyrated, thrust his pelvis, twirled the broom again. He was a good mover and he was having the time of his life. I stopped, transfixed; I wanted to shout, *Good on you!* I wanted to join in, I wanted to move and shake just like him, but I could only stand perfectly still, in bedazzled admiration.

When the music stopped, he saw me staring at him, and for one embarrassing moment, I thought he might lecture me for being rude. Instead, he doffed his council hat, made a flamboyant bow from the waist, and grinned up at me: 'At your service, my dear,' he said in mock-courtly fashion, amused by my stock-stillness, my gaping mouth. As I started to move away, sheepishly, he called after me: 'Another performance next Monday, lovely lady, same time, same place.' I couldn't stop myself from turning around to give him—much to my amazement—a girlish wave.

I returned home in a state of considerable perturbation. I was jittery, I was stirred up, I was all on fire. Hugo was not at home, thank goodness. He had gone, as he always did on a Monday, to visit his mother. (I haven't spoken of her before, but we shall come to her shortly, since we must.) I put the groceries away, trying to calm my nerves, subdue this not unwelcome agitation in my body. Milk in the fridge, bread in the breadbasket, bananas in the fruit bowl. That was easy. But still my stomach was fluttery, my limbs quivery. I picked up the broom to concentrate my mind on higher things, when suddenly I found myself dancing, dancing with the broom, in graceful dips and twirls, a modern waltz, whirling round and round the kitchen, my body lithe and sinuous, my hair pins falling out. I was glamorous, I was gorgeous, I was sexy, I was moving in a way I hadn't moved for years. My broom was Fred Astaire, I was Ginger Rogers in sparkling high heels. I was Cyd Charisse, shaking my booty; an enslaving Salome, a Gipsy Rose Lee, all long-legged freedom and veils of delight. I think I must have danced for hours.

Of course, on the following Monday, I took exactly the same path, the route I always took on my way home from shopping. The time couldn't come fast enough; how I endured that week I'll never know. So there I was, in front of the council building, in front of the same three men, with the same music pumping in the background. To cut a long story short, that's how I met Stan. I was bold, I was brazen: I made a move. I introduced myself and told him that I loved the way he danced. I remember my exact words: *I love the way you dance.* And I remember, exactly, what he replied: *I'd be even better if I was dancing with you.* (Yes, he knows it's a corny line, but as he told me later, he was *a bit out of practice.*) I asked Stan the name of the song to which he'd danced, and you'll be tickled to know it was the Village People's 'Macho Man'. (Stan the Macho Man became one of our many jokes.)

Will you be shocked to learn that a week later I moved out of the marital home and moved in with Stan? My mother-in-law certainly was. As a woman in her nineties, she thought her longevity both proof of moral probity and a justification for interfering in other people's lives. Needless to say, she told me that I was *a lost cause.* She expostulated, hyperventilated, ranted and raved: whatever it is people say and do when their moral order is severely shaken, if not destroyed, by the spectacle of a seventy-year-old woman refusing to act her age. *A disgrace to the family name, disgusting, a dereliction of duty,* you've heard it all before. My husband was less forthcoming. He roused himself enough to complain that *this was all the thanks he got for years of sacrifice and devotion,* but in the end I think he was simply too worn out to care very much at all. When he died three months later, my mother-in-law, with comic predictability, accused me of murdering her son. I saw no point in arguing. Besides, I thought, Hugo had been dead in all but name for much of his adult life.

Stan and I are still very happy together. We don't go dancing much these days; Stan's lumbago has been playing up and his arthritis is wearing out his knees. Nevertheless, he's still quite a nifty mover; after ten years of widowhood, he hasn't lost his touch. He always goes out on a Tuesday night for a poker game with the boys from the council (they tell him they can't believe his luck). I enjoy this time alone, especially the ritual of the evening meal. I always take the trouble to set the table nicely: the best crockery and cutlery, a linen napkin, roses in a vase. A three-course meal, with a glass of wine, two if I'm feeling up for it. I usually have soup to begin with, then fish or veal and potato croquettes, followed by crème caramel or fruit for dessert. And it will come as no surprise to you, I'm sure, that I take great pleasure not only in the cuisine but also, and especially, in slurping, slopping, stuffing and gobbling to my heart's content. Stan isn't there to see me, and even if he was, I know he wouldn't care.

Acknowledgements

I want to thank Terri-ann White, the Director of the University of Western Australia Press, for her enthusiastic support of new writing in general and the short story in particular. Her championing of the various pleasures and challenges of the genre is greatly appreciated. I also want to thank Linda Martin at UWA Press for her editorial incisiveness, sensitivity and professionalism.

Gail Jones has been enormously encouraging in many ways. I am very grateful for her intelligent and subtle responses to these stories and for many cherished years of stimulating literary discussion and magnificently supportive friendship. I also thank my dear friends Victoria Burrows and Prue Kerr for their unfailing generosity and kindness over many years, their social artistry and dancing down corridors.

Heartfelt thanks to my mother for her stories—sometimes harrowing, sometimes amusing—about family life.

My two sons, Jack and Harry, have been interested spectators in the process of writing and I thank them for this, and for the gift of their creativity, intelligence and keenly ironic sense of humour.

Dan Midalia has made this collection of stories possible in both intangible and practical ways. I thank him for his patience and unflagging sense of optimism, and for postponing his retirement so that I could have a proper space for writing. I am deeply grateful for his support and for the love which informs it.

Also in the New Writing series

Scottish purveyor of erudite filth ... you're gonna love Ewan Morrison's debut collection.
Arena

THE LAST BOOK YOU READ
and other stories

Ewan Morrison

New Writing

ISBN 978 0 9802964 7 1

Frank, witty, disturbing and ultimately compassionate, *The Last Book You Read* marks the Australian debut of a powerful new voice in world literature. Scottish author Ewan Morrison's no-holds-barred collection of short stories tells of people caught between places and lovers as well as between desire, addiction and regret.

...the most compelling Scottish literary debut since Irvine Welsh's Trainspotting.
– *The Sunday Times (London)*

Available now at all good bookstores or order online at www.uwapress.uwa.edu.au
Tel: 08 6488 3670   E-mail: admin@uwapress.uwa.edu.au